We hadn't gone a block when I spotted a black car with a cracked passenger side mirror. "Adrian..."

"I see it." There was something odd in his voice. Some anger, some resignation. "Stay slightly behind me."

"Okay." The car came to a stop. "Um, any ideas?" I asked, mentally cataloging the nearest public buildings. The storefront next to us was closed, but there was a gas station about fifty yards behind us, and a library across the street. The café was only a little further back.

"I think I know what this is about." He turned his back on the car, put his left hand over his right, and ran his hand down his fingers. A sign we had invented. Follow my lead. *Then he took his right hand, crossed his first two fingers, and tapped his collar bone briefly.* Intimidation, not yet threat. Act calm. *If he had used three fingers, tapping twice, it would have meant,* Intimidation, not yet threat. Act scared.

I scratched twice at my ear. Message received.

He turned back, muttering under his breath, "Be prepared to run if need be."

Books by H. J. Harding

Moonlit Memories Series:

Secrets of the Moon Fox

Nightmare's Revenge

The Hyde Chronicles:

The Pawn's Play

Knightfall

The Bishop's Decoy

THE BISHOP'S DECOY

The Hyde Chronicles: Book Three

By H. J. Harding

This is a work of fiction. Any resemblance to real people or events is a coincidence. Some places were borrowed, but were returned more or less intact. Hyde University is fictional, much to my dismay. If it really existed, it would be run with much more competence. If you actually read this, please email the author at **hjhardingbooks@gmail.com** and let me know.

Acknowledgements

Every book that exists has multiple parents. Thank you to Katie who wanted me to write this in the first place, and will someday read one of my books. Thank you to Wallace who fell in love with the universe and believes me one of the best writers in the world. Sometimes, anyway.

Thank you to everyone who read this book in its' early stages, particularly my editor, Petticoat Betty.

Thank you to everyone who reads this book, buys this book, or tells someone else to buy this book. If you've done all three, thank you thrice.

Last but certainly not least, thank you to my Lord and Savior. Nothing can be accomplished without you and if it could, it would be meaningless. May this book honor You.

Chapter One

Classroom Antics

"The Roommate Request forms are here," Ilse said as she walked in the room, slips of paper in her hand. "I have yours."

I looked up from my textbook. "Already? Isn't it a little early?"

"It's almost March. The term ends in mid-April. It takes time to match up roommates properly." Ilse handed me one of the forms.

"I can imagine." Personally, I was very grateful it wasn't my job to match up living arrangements for multiple beings from multiple dimensions. I'm sure it got very complicated. "Hard to believe the year is almost over." It had been quite a year, even if things had calmed down lately. No one was trying to kill me at the moment, for one. That I knew of anyway. College was definitely a broadening experience.

"I would think you'd be relieved." Ilse took the pen I handed her with a regal nod of thanks. "If you are not opposed, I intend to request you as my roommate next year as well."

"That's fine. I was going to request you, too." The paper asked for second choice also. "I think I'll put Kara down as my second choice. She'd probably prefer to stay with Denise, but…"

"Then I shall mention Denise as my second choice. Though I do not believe we need be concerned. Those who request each other are frequently granted their request."

As much as Ilse liked Kara, I could understand why she would not be eager to room with the Werewolf. Kara was too hyper, energetic, and social for Ilse's more reserved tastes. Denise, Kara's current roommate, was a dragonfly shifter from the Bahamas, and a much more laid back, quiet personality. I took the pen back from Ilse and used it to fill out my own form.

Name: Violet Peters. **Current Room:** Price 613. **Gender:** Female. **Species:** Human. **Roommate Requests (Include Name and Species): First choice:** Ilse Teps (Vampire). **Second Choice:** Kara Furton (Werewolf). **Housing Needs:** Standard Land Based.

"You seem deep in thought," Ilse said as I fell silent after filling out the form.

"I'm thinking about summer."

"Ah, are you looking forward to returning home? Seeing your family again?"

"Honestly? Not really. Christmas break was awful. I couldn't tell them about the school, and they couldn't understand that, or why I changed. Mom and I were constantly fighting, and we've never done that before. Now Jesse will be there, and…"

My cousin Jesse was going to be a problem. He had come to Hyde University and learned about the dimensions and the different beings from those dimensions. We both signed a magical contract not to share this information with those who hadn't signed the contract and weren't 'in the know'. Like our families. However, Jesse decided that staying at Hyde wasn't worth it. Not worth dealing with the secrets, not worth the prejudice, not worth family tension, and not worth dealing with those who wanted us gone so badly they were willing to resort to potentially lethal means. I couldn't blame Jesse for making the choice he did, but I can't leave Hyde. If there was one person I really wasn't looking forward to seeing, it was my cousin Jesse.

"Perhaps you are focusing on the wrong things." Ilse pulled me from my thoughts.

"What do you mean?"

"Perhaps, instead of focusing on the secrets and what you cannot tell your family, you should focus on what you can. You have a camera. Take pictures of the room, your friends who can pass as human, pictures of campus when and where you can. Certainly you can take pictures of the village across the lake."

"Huh, I hadn't thought of that. Good idea, Ilse." Hyde University was on an island in Wollaston Lake, Saskatchewan. On the shores of Wollaston Lake is a small town, also called Wollaston Lake. However, while the island is a nexus point between all known major dimensions, the town isn't part of that. The people there were presumably all, or at least mostly, human.

"You would have eventually." Despite her dismissive comment, Ilse smiled at the praise. "Do make certain that you and your cousin compare notes. You need to know what he informed your family."

I nodded. It probably wouldn't take care of all the tension, not by a long shot. But almost anything would be better than Christmas. "I may also sign up for one of the summer courses." There were two summer mini-terms. One was from May to mid-June, the other was July to mid-August, which was when the official term started. A short time home would probably be better.

"Do try to keep from becoming estranged from your family. You did say you were close when you started."

I sighed but didn't say anything. It wasn't that I liked the new tension between us, but they would never understand and I couldn't tell them. "What time is it?"

"Almost twelve-thirty. We should probably go."

Grabbing my coat, I stood and followed her out of the room. We took the stairs from the sixth floor to the ground floor, dropping off the roommate request forms with the RA on duty. It was Thylica the wood elf, who happened to be our RA.

The weather was cold, like usual, but not so bad that we decided to take the underground tunnels that ran across the island. Ilse didn't seem as vulnerable to the cold as I was, so she did ask me what I wanted to do first. But while the weather was a balmy seventeen degrees, I was getting better at the cold. Besides, the night was still, and the library close by.

Our walk to King library was silent. Once inside, we separated, with Ilse browsing the shelves near the check-out counter, under Ms. Grazletz, the dragon head librarian's, suspicious gaze. I tried to be as inconspicuous as I could while walking to where the elevator was right now. It moved when no one was looking, but it was always marked on the map which could be called up at any time.

I was grateful that Ilse was willing to play decoy. Ms. Graz didn't like me very much. Or trust me, at all. That I could tell anyway. Not since the explosion in the library. That hadn't even been my fault. Not really.

Regardless of the blame, I was usually trying to avoid Ms. Graz, because she still seems to think I'm up to something. Then again, technically, we are.

Tim, a yeti, was already in a study room. We hadn't specified exactly which one we'd meet in, because that was just asking for Murphy, Imp of Spite, to interfere. Okay, I don't think Murphy's Law was a real being, which I had been forced to specify a few times. But there were times I wondered. First one there saved the room. Krystal and Bria, twin Ice Elementals who shared the room next to us, made it to the room just before I got there, probably because I had paused to grab a couple random books. I glanced down to see what books I had picked. 'Music in Magic' and 'The History of Murderous Plants', apparently. Odd that those were in the same section. Then again, even after nearly a school year, I still hadn't figured out the cataloging system.

Ilse arrived while we were still greeting each other and spreading the books around for camouflage. Kara and Denise were a minute or two behind her, with Kara giving an in-depth description of her last Ultimate Frisbee Deathmatch game. I was told that no one actually died during those games, but from what I could tell the few times I watched, it wasn't from lack of trying. I honestly couldn't tell if Denise was interested, thinking about something else, or sleep walking with her eyes open. Never could read Denise well.

That just left the Chars. I knew Adrian had night classes, but he shouldn't have one right now, or we wouldn't have scheduled a meeting for this time. Allison was an alumna and her schedule was pretty open except when she was working on the Celebration Committee. They were currently working on the Spring Dance, but she wouldn't have meetings after midnight. Well, unless the committee is mostly made up of nocturnal beings.

Allison beat her brother to the room, taking a seat where she could see through the window to make sure no one was watching us too closely. "Adrian's on his way. He's just feeling a little paranoid. Wants to sweep the floor, make sure no one's too close."

"But there haven't been any problems in weeks, right?" Kara asked.

"No, but we know it isn't over." Personally, I could appreciate Adrian's paranoia. He was just barely healed from the last attack. I hoped he had fully healed anyway. He still seemed to move stiffly sometimes. More worryingly, Adrian was a defender psychic. If he was worried, it might not be just paranoia.

Adrian sauntered in a few minutes later, reminiscent of his black panther form. He spotted Allison taking vantage point and nodded, looking satisfied. Two taps to the window fogged the glass, giving us a little privacy. Any faculty member or staff could make the glass clear again, but we would be safe from students lip-reading us at least.

He took a free chair and sat sideways so he could see most of the table and the crack under the door at the same time. "There's too many of us. Too noticeable a group. Especially if we keep meeting in the library. We aren't even in the same year."

There were nine of us. Tim, being an eight or so foot tall yeti, was going to attract attention no matter what. Even for Hyde, he was one of the larger beings. Adrian was a sophomore who had gotten into enough trouble last year to have been the center of a thousand rumors. Allison was an alumni who was often in the middle of special events. The rest of us, including Tim, were all freshmen. We had different majors, different classes, we didn't even share a species or a dimension. Meeting at the library once a week or so, yeah, we may have attracted notice. "Is it people *have* noticed, or *will* notice if we keep it up?"

"There have been a few questions." Adrian briefly made eye contact with me before going back to watching the door.

"Then there isn't much point in changing." When everyone looked at me, I shrugged. "If they are already noticing, then they'll notice if we stop. Besides, we hang out other times too."

"It might not be a bad idea to vary where we meet." Ilse looked at the glass like she was trying to peer through the fog. "Alas, that would be easier determined than accomplished."

Adrian and Tim weren't permitted in our dorm, or vice versa. We might be allowed in Allison's room, since alumni had different rules, but her room was barely bigger than this study room, and the furniture made it smaller. Class rooms were kept locked when not in use. There were a few study rooms underneath the dorms where students could meet, but we had been using one of those before the door blew up. Then we disappeared before we were blamed for *that*.

"Well, we can think about different places we could meet. Perhaps meet in smaller groups," Allison suggested.

We still hadn't figured out if we would get in trouble if the staff found out what we were doing. Yes, we were trying to save the school, but we had also been told to leave the matter alone. Well, it had been heavily implied. Besides, we weren't sure who could be trusted. It was possible, maybe even probable, that there was at least one member of the staff working to shut down the school.

Hyde University, as we discovered last October, was dependent of keeping an oath. Among other things sworn, was the clause that there would always be at least one human, one vampire, one shifter, one elemental, and Taria at the school. Taria was an immortal, only one known of her kind, who helped found the school and was known for her verging on creepy devotion to the school.

If the school faltered on this oath, it might well be forced to close. Which appeared to be someone's intention. Taria had no intention of leaving, and there were plenty of vampires, shifters, and elementals. But I was the only human in the entire school right now. Jesse didn't last a full month, and I didn't know how much luck they were having in finding any others.

My friends and I swore our own oath. To be loyal to the school and each other; to keep the school open and running. This was a little complicated, especially since our oath included obeying the teachers, and we were skirting that by even meeting like this to try to uncover who was behind this conspiracy. But our oath also wouldn't let us stop and ignore the problems either.

"So does anyone have anything new?" I asked.

"We were looking into who used the land before the University was built," Kara spoke up, indicating herself, her twin sister Bria, and Denise. "The Mers from 8D say the climate has changed enough that they wouldn't be able to use the area anymore. Not the land itself, anyway; and they don't seem particularly interested in the water. The Frostfire dragon clan is small, less than three thousand known individuals. They moved areas eons ago. The Yetis are a bigger group, but similar story. Bria is still looking into the frost sprites."

"I'm not sure we can rule out a group just because they've left the area," I mused. "Nothing says they can't move back."

There were a few agreements. "We should see who in the school belongs to those groups." Krystal looked up from drawing snowflakes on the table with ice residue. "Tim, I know you…"

"No, I understand. I do not believe any of my kind are involved in our current troubles, but we should, of course, be certain. There are very few yeti on campus. It should not be difficult for me to… become better acquainted with them." Tim gave what was probably supposed to be a smile.

"Worth remembering, none of the people we've had trouble with so far have been from any of those groups." Adrian kept staring at the door. "We don't know how many others have been cajoled, hoodwinked, or brainwashed into being part of this."

I tried very, very hard not to shiver. Yes, I remembered, all too well, what someone tricked or brainwashed could do.

"So we'll keep our eyes open," Allison said.

"And stick together," Kara added.

That led nicely into a discussion of roommate request forms. Kara and Denise hadn't filled their forms out yet, and were nothing loathe to putting Ilse and I as their second choices. Krystal and Bria, being twins, wanted to stay together but did agree to consider putting some of us down as second choices. Adrian and Tim preferred to stay with their current roommates, and didn't want to share a room with each other. Probably just as well. While a lot of progress had been made, those two still only got along about half the time. Allison, being an alumna living in alumni housing, actually had her own room. Not that it was much better than we had.

She shared a bathroom with whoever had the room next to her, whereas the rest of us had a set of rooms. Ilse and I, like all roommates, shared a sitting room and a bathroom, and each had our own bedrooms. Kara said the college was built that way to prevent fatalities. I don't know if she was right, but I certainly wasn't complaining about having my own space. I hadn't even shared a room with my sister, Rose, in years.

The meeting ended soon after that. Ilse had class, Adrian might have too. We made plans to meet again next week, with alternate ideas on where we could meet. Sneaking around got hard, but it seemed to still be necessary.

***

My friends and I may have been making a concentrated effort to keep someone from closing the school, but that didn't mean we had an excuse to get out of our school work. In fact, the oath *we* swore included following the principles the school was founded on. It was only in retrospect we realized that we hadn't known for certain what principles the school *was* founded on. It took time to find the original code of conduct:

I swear to maintain discipline, academically, physically, and mentally; to abandon intolerance and embrace understanding. I swear to be loyal to the school and my home, obey my superiors, and defend the school as necessary. I will strive for peace, but prepare for conflict. I will do my best to be my best.

Magically enforced oaths can be a pain. Ours knew when we were slacking. I think all of us had at least once or twice felt pain or ill because the oath judged that we weren't doing our best in one of those areas. I got headaches if I put off my homework. Adrian once had what seemed like a nasty case of food poisoning for getting in a fight. Interestingly enough, I didn't suffer any noticeable consequences for yelling at him and his opponent over the same incident. So far we didn't know if that meant the oath didn't care about verbal fights or if magic thought I was justified in my anger.

Thinking about the oath, it would probably be best if Tim and Adrian weren't rooming together. I'm not sure they could get along well enough in small quarters to keep the oath satisfied. Which could result in them being sick often enough that they couldn't keep on top of their schoolwork. Vicious cycle there.

Anyway, because both the oath and Dr. Kraes, my professor for Prominent Forms of Government, demanded it, I had a debate today. In front of my whole government class, I had to defend the idea that the governed should know the identities and character of those who governed them. I had picked that topic because I thought it would be easy. Of *course* we should know who is making the laws and enforcing them.

Perhaps unsurprisingly, that very attitude made coming up with an argument harder than I expected. It was something taken for granted in 13A, my dimension. Human history didn't have a real precedent of *not* knowing who the rulers were. Sure there was talk of secret societies or individuals that were pulling strings behind the scenes, and some might even be true, but there was always someone people could point to and say 'That person's in charge.' Even if they weren't always correct.

It was almost like arguing that being to breathe was a good thing. How did someone come up with supporting evidence for something they took for granted every day? I had to do a lot of research into other places and governments where the governed didn't know the identities of the rulers, and knew they didn't know. The primary example was the Inter-Dimensional Council. A select cabal of individuals, one from each dimension cluster (one from the 1s, one from the 2s, etc.), who, once voted in, stayed for life unless impeached by two-thirds of the council, and whose identity was never known to the average person. Ilse couldn't name her representative, even though she voted in the last election. Instead of the candidates being named, they were described. Qualifications, species, etc. Ilse said she was pretty sure the representatives for the 12s is currently a vampire, but she didn't know. They didn't say who won.

A hundred years after the member's death or retirement, their name might be released, depending on the wishes of the family. There were stories of even family members being shocked to find out their husband, wife, mother, father, child, or sibling served on the council.

For people like me, who originally came from shade dimensions, a dimension where less than a quarter of the population knew about the dimensions and other beings from them, and it was illegal to tell anyone not in the know; the Inter-dimensional Council was something we learned about quickly. Ilse explained it to me on my first day, and it was covered during orientation.

My opponent, which was probably not a good thing, was Arie, the harpy who lived two doors down from me on my floor. Next to Krystal and Bria. Arie was… difficult for me to get along with. I thought she hated me because I was human. Apparently it was a lot more complicated than that. She believed my grades were being artificially inflated and I believed she was a prejudiced snob. As it turns out, my grades probably aren't being adjusted and she's just a snob.

Arie claims she doesn't hate me, and it has nothing to do with me being human, but we certainly aren't exchanging friendship bracelets. Which would be fine, except Arie likes Tim. Really likes Tim. And Tim very much seems to like Arie. Which meant the two of us had to at least try to pretend to get along.

Because the two of us were debating each other, Tim, my only friend in class, was torn between who to root for. Which wasn't surprising at all, but I really wished I had his support in this.

Dr. Kraes called us both to the front. Dr. Kraes was a Solurt. One of many types of beings I hadn't even heard of before I got to Hyde. Solurts look like walking beams of light and neither have nor recognize gender. They would get offended if referred to as 'he' or 'she', preferring 'it' which they also used for all others.

It stood before the class. "Indicate if you believe that beings should know the identities of those in government in all cases." There were a few scattered responses, generally by raising a hand or similar appendage. One Solurt brightened and dimmed in a short pulse, and there were a few musical trills that I couldn't tell the origin of. "Now indicate if you believe there are times when the identities of those in government should be hidden from the general populace." More responses, pretty much of the same kinds. Unless I was mistaken, about a quarter of the class didn't respond at all. "Violet, you have first point."

Mentally thanking Ilse for her insights and for helping me practice, I took my two minutes, mentioning briefly the importance of governments being accountable to the people, the need for oversight, an informed voting body, and how could change happen if the people didn't know who needed to be changed. Ilse had helped me find enough examples in various dimensions so I wasn't just falling back on what I knew.

Then Arie got to question me. She pointed out how even when there was a chance, many voters were uninformed. That change was often violent. Why did we need oversight if people were elected for life? The risk of assassination, etc.

Then she made her points and I questioned her. It was much the same material. Then there were our final rebuttals. I didn't know if I was changing anyone's mind, but I would be satisfied with not looking like an idiot.

At the end, Dr. Kraes again questioned the class on their stances. While most still agreed with Arie's position, there were clearly a few more who sided with me than there was in the beginning.

By the time I got to my seat, I felt like I might collapse. But I took my seat next to Tim, smiling when he told me I did a good job. Of course, he told Arie the same thing. Then again, she *did* do a good job. At least I didn't fumble too badly. I so owed Ilse. If she actually ate, I'd buy her some ice cream or something. I'd have to think about it.

Class was dismissed as we were assured we would have our grades given in the next class. I said a quick goodbye to Tim that might or might not have included Arie and dashed off to Genetics.

Intro to Genetics was my favorite class this semester, and a cornerstone of my major; Biology with a concentration in genetics. Dr. Gronk, the troll professor, was also my favorite teacher. I had him for Bio I, and was currently taking Bio II with him along with genetics. If I was lucky, I could take Zoology with him next semester. I still had a week until I could register for classes and was a little worried the class might be full before then. The closer you were to graduating, the more you were given priority. As a freshman, I was pretty much bottom of the heap. Oh well, no point worrying about it now.

Dr. Gronk, normally a bright orange color, seemed to be covered with pink zebra stripes and chartreuse polka dots. Since none of my research in trolls indicated any ability to change their scale color, I guessed he had fallen prey to the Science Department's endless prank war. He was one of the main instigators in said prank war, so it wasn't much of a surprise.

Whatever his feelings about his current coloring, Dr. Gronk was acting completely normal. It was conceivably possible that he didn't know, but I doubted that was the case.

Today we were turning in the second of three major papers we had to do for the class. Mine was 'The History of Observed Inherited Traits'. Basically, how genetics was discovered and tracked in different dimensions prior to the invention of technology to observe DNA. The hard part had been limiting what to put in the paper.

I had been interested in the subject even before ninth grade biology. I even named my teddy bear Mendel after Gregor Mendel, father of genetics. Now there were a lot more dimensions who had their own history of observing and guessing how traits were passed on. Books could be written on the subject. And had been.

Mendel probably still got a little more time than he should have, but I did limit him to three-quarters of a page. But I only spent a paragraph on how vampires had deduced blood related hereditary illnesses and the three main scientists or doctors that discovered that. This was a ten page paper, and I had done an eight page paper on Mendel back in ninth grade. I could probably do twenty pages on him now, easy.

Hyde University library had information about him that was forgotten in my home dimension. Not to mention all the other information I could find there. I think I would probably try to practically live in the library if it didn't mean being under hostile eyes all the time. Well, and the bookshelves that tried to trap you. And the nasty, awful, evil, homicidal Staircases of Doom. Okay, maybe it's a good thing I'm not living in the library.

I was a lot more confident in my paper than I was in my speech. It's easier to gather my thoughts writing than speaking, and Ilse proofread my reports.

We had developed a system. I typed all of our papers, and Ilse edited them. I was the faster typist, and Ilse had a tendency to write everything longhand. Luckily, part of vampire aristocracy training was in readable, elegant handwriting. Also luckily, even disregarding the language spell that allows us to hear, read, and speak the languages around us with about ninety-five percent accuracy, Ilse knew English. Not the American version as much, and a somewhat old fashioned version, but still, English. Which meant there was less likelihood of those five percent inaccuracies. Like when I asked Bria about her shirt and she told me something about ducks. Never did figure out what happened there.

I'd say that the spell might explain some of what Denise says, but she actually is speaking English. She's from my dimension, the Bahamas, to be exact. Maybe I could visit her there someday. It would have to be way warmer than this college that was built closer to the Arctic Circle than sensible humans had any decent reason to be. No, I'm not bitter about the freezing weather, constant snow for the last five months, ice everywhere, or the fact that I nearly froze to death at least once, or… Okay, maybe a little bitter.

In my defense, when I first arrived here, my hometown of Newport News, Virginia, had been in the nineties all week, flirting with the triple digits. That was August. Wollaston Lake, at that same time, was under sixty degrees. I've built up some cold tolerance since then, some magically, some naturally, and some by acquiring warmer clothing. But it would be a lie to say I liked the cold.

Which was why I was currently huddled in my coat, even in the classroom. This particular classroom had a semi open air porch for flyers. There was some weather protection, I suspect magical in origin, but the room was still at least fifteen degrees colder than the hallway and most other classrooms. Oh well, into every life some rain must fall. And to be honest, compared to some of the other things I've had to deal with at Hyde, cold classrooms are a breeze. Perhaps literally.

"Reports on my desk before you leave the classroom. As another reminder, which you shouldn't need, paper is the preferred medium. Papyrus, parchment, and clay or wax tablets are permissible. Collages using feathers, sticks, stones, etc. are discouraged, and I'm afraid I can't read bubble. I will accept electronic format, if it is received by my computer before four o'clock this afternoon." Dr. Gronk repeated his customary warning he gave at the start and finish of every written assignment. I thought it was a joke the first time, but I have since seen students bring in fish tanks to report in bubble. In a different class, I saw someone turn in a collage for a report and then argue with the teacher about what every element stood for. In fact, I had seen every single medium he mentioned used at least once, and one or two others besides.

Class went well, with a rousing discussion of sex-linked recessive traits. As class ended, students trailed out dropping off their reports on Dr. Gronk's desk. Realizing I didn't have my paper out, I started rooting through my backpack for it. Then I went searching again. And again. Where was my paper?

Chapter Two

Loves, Likes, and Loyalties

I didn't realize I was biting my lip until the pain struck. I could not have lost my paper. I simply could *not* have. Where was it?

I finished it last night, Ilse edited it, and I printed it. I remembered using a blue binder clip to hold it together and putting it in my notebook so it didn't get crumpled. But it wasn't in my notebook. It wasn't on my desk or on the floor around the desk. Where could it be?

"Violet?"

I gasped, looking up at Dr. Gronk. Everyone else had left and I was the last one there. The troll professor eyed me with concern. "Is something wrong?"

"My paper! I can't find it. I had it, I know I did. I wrote it, printed it last night. My roommate read it too, she edited it. It was in my backpack, but I can't find it!" Tears were starting to slip out. That paper was worth a fifth of my grade! Four o'clock was only five minutes away. I wouldn't even be able to back to my room in time if I started running now.

"Okay, take a deep breath. Good, another." I did. "You're a good student. I believe you wrote your paper. You've been on time with everything else, and your assignments have always been well-written. You are in Price Hall, right?"

I nodded. My throat was too tight to speak.

"Do you have a class this period?"

I shook my head.

"You said you printed it out. That means you typed it up. Did you save it?" I nodded vigorously. Always, always save your work. I lived by that rule.

"Good. You go to your room and email me your paper. As long as I get it within half an hour, I'll count it as on time. Okay?"

"Thank you! I don't know what happened."

Dr. Gronk looked grave. "I think you might."

I sighed at that. Yeah, I did. If I had put it in my backpack last night and it was gone now, it probably had some help disappearing. I knew I wasn't well-liked, but usually that resulted in low level harassment, or someone trying to put me in danger so I'd leave. Not trying to make me fail.

"Any suspects?"

"No." I truly didn't have a clue. Even if I did, I would have wanted some evidence before I said anything.

"Okay. Go email me your paper."

"I will. Thank you again." I dashed out the room. Adrian was waiting for me. He often hung around outside various classes of mine. "Can't talk, have to get back to Price."

He easily kept pace with my brisk walk. "Any particular reason?"

"My paper went missing." Out of the corner of my eye, I could see Adrian's wince. He knew how much that paper was worth too. And that my scholarship required me to keep my grades up. "Dr. Gronk believes it wasn't my fault and will count it as on time if I can email him a copy within a half-hour."

"Nice of him."

I nodded. We were on the stairs now, and I was taking them a little too fast to want to try talking. We took the tunnels under the school, both for warmth and speed. I might have been able to sneak Adrian into the dorm from here, but that would be against the rules. And there might even be precautions against it, who knows? Instead, I summoned the elevator. "I can come back after I email my paper. I just…"

"Go. I'll wait here."

Since it was daytime, if not exactly daylight, more twilight, Ilse was asleep. Didn't matter. The computer was in the sitting room. I was flustered enough that I mistyped my password twice, but I finally got on and found my paper. I quickly checked that this was the copy I had printed, before emailing a copy to Dr. Gronk.

And was immediately told it didn't go through. I sent it again, making sure I was using the right address. Was it going through? Everything was so sluggish I couldn't tell. Not willing to risk it, I printed off another copy.

Adrian gave me a look as he saw the papers in my hand and that I was in just as much hurry as before.

"Email's acting up. This way I can give him a physical copy."

He nodded, once again keeping pace easily as if I wasn't practically jogging. Which was not a major surprise, since Adrian was in better physical shape than I was. Though I was better than I had been. The oath required us to keep up regular exercise routines. I was better off than some, since I had played lacrosse in high school and had kept fit from that.

So I was out of breath, but not falling down when I got back to Dr. Gronk's office. The still pink and chartreuse troll looked up at me in surprise.

"Email." I gasped, then tried again. "The email network seems to be down. I didn't trust it. Here." I handed over my printed copy.

"Oh, thank you. I wondered if something was off. I suppose I shall have to be a little more lenient with my students today."

I felt, more than saw Adrian come up behind me. If I wasn't mistaken, I also felt some of his surprise and amusement. Possible, thanks to the oath, we had started to share some emotions on occasion. But most of them were bad emotions. Fear, sadness, something that said we needed help. This was a bit new.

Dr. Gronk spotted Adrian and seemed to recognize him. That could be a problem. Adrian was still on disciplinary probation. "Ah, Mister... Char. Wasn't it?"

"Yes?" Adrian said, backing up slightly.

"You participated in the New Year's talent show, if I remember right. Sang."

Oh, yes. He did. I had forgotten about that. Dr. Gronk ran a talent show where, in addition to the people who signed up, he would pick on random audience members to perform.

"Yes, yes I did." Apparently Adrian hadn't been thinking about that either.

"You are quite good, young man."

"Thanks?"

"You *are* good. I got chills." I really had. He sang 'Who wants to live forever', which can get me emotional on a good day, but he was wonderful.

Adrian shrugged and studied the rug. Since it was the same exact gray carpet flecked with black and white specks that was every carpet on campus, I doubted it was that interesting.

"Listen to the young lady. You have a talent." Dr. Gronk smiled. "Of course, I was really calling on you," He said, looking at me.

Even remembering how nervous I had been, I blushed. "I... I couldn't. I just... I don't have those kinds of talents."

"She said if you called on her, she'd faint. Not a good recommendation for your show. I did tell her that fainting on command was a talent, but she didn't believe me." Now that we weren't talking about his singing, Adrian was a little more confident. He was also reciting a conversation from a couple months ago with great accuracy.

Dr. Gronk laughed. "Then I apologize. It was not my intent to cause distress. You never seemed shy about asking questions in class. Or answering them."

"I know what I'm talking about there. I know what I'm doing."

"True. Say, Mr. Char, I seem to recall seeing you in Dr. Jixryst's Organic Chemistry class. Would I be correct in my recollection?"

"Uh...yes?" I couldn't blame him for being hesitant to answer that one. *Everyone* knew about the science division prank wars, even if we didn't have evidence of it right in front of us. But usually the teachers left the students out of it for the most part.

"Would you perhaps be so kind as to deliver this file to the good Doctor on your way out of the building?" Dr. Gronk picked up a fat folder.

"What's it do?" Adrian eyed it like it was a snake ready to bite him.

Dr. Gronk laughed, like rocks rolling in water. "It

is not in any way tampered with, or would involve you in the amusements of the teachers' mischief. I give you my word."

That was good enough for me. I stepped forward to take it, even if I didn't know where Dr. Jixryst's office was, or even who or what Dr. Jixryst was. Before I could reach for it, Adrian cut me off and took the folder. "Okay, I'll take it over."

"Thank you ever so. It is good to see such manners in young people." Dr. Gronk grinned in such a way that I found myself wondering if I had somehow missed a joke. Oh, well. I got my paper turned in and wasn't penalized for being late, and Dr. Gronk didn't seem upset by Adrian trying to protect me from him. If he even realized.

"Well, have good day, Dr. Gronk. Thank you for letting me turn in my paper."

Adrian just nodded.

"You are most welcome. Glad you were able to print a new copy." He eyed the cover. "Observed traits? Good. That has a rich history. I look forward to reading it."

Was I blushing? Probably a little. Adrian was smirking at me, which was a good indication. I took a leaf out of Adrian's book; nodded, smiled, and backed out of the room.

Adrian sauntered after me. "We need to stop by the second floor."

"Is that where Dr. Jixryst's office is?"

"Yeah, near the east staircase." Adrian led the way unerringly. Made sense, he was a Chemistry major and a sophomore. He had probably been here before.

Dr. Jixryst's office was in a corner, near one of the labs. Adrian knocked on the door labeled Tickla Jixryst. "Come in." The voice sounded female, but there was a rough quality to the voice, suggesting different vocal cords.

Adrian opened the door. "Hey, Dr. Jixryst. Dr. Gronk asked me to bring this over. He promised it wasn't pranked." He handed the file over. As he did so, I moved a little so I could see who he was handing it too.

Dr. Jixryst was indeed female. In fact, she was a female troll; aqua and teal scaled with hair in a color that simply wasn't in my normal color range. Purple-green was probably the closest equivalent.

The scales on her hands darkened some as she accepted the file. I was pretty sure that was the troll equivalent of a blush. Why would she blush, unless… oh. Oh! Maybe.

"Thank you. I appreciate the efforts."

"No problem."

We left then. I debated if I should, or even could ask Adrian if he agreed with my hunch. Well, maybe I could at least check my facts. "The hand scales darkening, that's a little like a blush for a troll, right?"

"Yeah." Adrian smirked.

"What's that for?"

"What's what for?"

"That smirk."

"Yes, she was blushing at the thought of your professor."

"Aww, that's cute." I smiled.

Adrian shook his head. "Girls."

"You don't think so?"

"If the feelings aren't returned then it's just awkward."

I winced. Point, definite point. "Oh, dear. Do you think Dr. Gronk…" How would Adrian know? What business was it of mine anyway?

"Oh, he does." He tapped his nose.

I managed not to squeal. "Then it's definitely cute."

Adrian shook his head again, but he was smiling. A little. I think. "You think it's cute too, I can tell." I frowned. "Do you think they are actually seeing each other, or stuck in the 'Do I say something or not?' stage?"

The panther shifter shrugged. "Don't know. Don't think it's my business."

"No, I guess it isn't." I sighed.

Adrian rubbed at the back of his head. "Um, I've been meaning to ask. Well, I'm going to the mainland this Saturday. Did, would you like to come with me?"

If this was Adrian's way of asking me out on a date, it needed a little work. We had dated a little bit, but neither of us really knew what to do. Adrian was a defender psychic and I was his primary bonded protectorate. This bond was for life, which was why defender psychics almost always married their primary bonded protectorate, unless they were siblings. I had done the research and knew the statistics. Allison said that Adrian hadn't done the research and didn't know the statistics, but he still knew it happened a lot. It was something I tried not to think about. That would just make things awkward.

I didn't really need to go to town. Unless... "Yes, I think I would like to come. I need to take some pictures."

He gave me a confused look. "Of the town?"

"Yes. Remember how I came back early during Christmas break?" Adrian frowned but nodded. "Most of my trouble was that I couldn't tell my family what was going on, or any details about Hyde. Ilse suggested I try to focus on what I can tell them. Take pictures of what I can show them; the town, my room, friends who look human, etc. Can I take your picture?"

Now Adrian was really frowning. I don't know what's going on in the Char family, but I do know Adrian was at the school all of last summer and over Christmas break. Allison went back and forth, but Adrian signed up classes, on his own admission, because they fit the schedule. Not necessarily because he needed them. When Allison suddenly joined the alumni association, Adrian asked if she had come to spy on him. She did admit that part of her job was to keep an eye out for him. Then, when Adrian got badly hurt, to the point he actually clinically died at least once, his parents never came by to visit him. So I generally tried not to complain about my family issues to him. Or discuss family much at all, if possible.

Then again, he might just not like having his picture taken. "You told your family about me?"

"Of course." Probably best not to tell him that I first mentioned him back when he was still stalking me and I didn't know why. "So, may I?"

Adrian shrugged. "I guess. If you really want." He seemed to be holding back from making a face.

"Don't like pictures? I don't like getting my picture taken either."

"Dad's in politics. There were a lot of cameras. A whole lot of cameras." The low lying venom in his voice was almost frightening.

"I can understand that. I wouldn't enjoy it either. Fishbowl life." I suppressed a shiver. I got stared at enough here.

That made Adrian smile, at least. "Don't visit my

home, then."

Okay, that might eventually be an issue; but I wasn't going to worry about it now. "Duly noted." Maybe I could get a picture of him making balloon animals for the kids. Hmm, I'd have to go through my pictures before I showed them to anyone. After all, I had some pictures of my trip to the North Pole. Those could be a little difficult to explain. It was an awesome trip though. Tim's family had invited us. Pity I couldn't invite everyone to visit me. But it simply wasn't possible.

***

Every single semester, or school year, I try to keep on top of things, stay organized, and be prepared for exams and final projects. Even when I'm counting down the days, there arises a point where it's like finals week suddenly jumps out and shouts, 'Here I am!' It hadn't arrived yet, but it was rapidly approaching. Final papers and projects were coming due. We had to move out of our dorms, which I was really not looking forward to, and I had to take all my stuff back home, which I was looking forward to even less. I was in a photo taking frenzy, because other things had always come up, and it simply hadn't been a major priority.

Ilse had let me take her picture, as had both the Chars, Kara, Denise, and a few others in the hall: Sylvia, a snake shifter; Cal, a wind elemental; Felicity, a werecat; and Bria. Krystal was a little more camera shy, and I didn't want to explain why both the identical twins had identical blue tinged blonde hair. Once, it was hair dye. Twice... well, it might seem a little odd. Professor Collins, the magicus who teaches Magic for Non-magic

Users, also let me take a picture and even cast an illusion over the class room so it was safe to photograph.

I took a few careful pictures of the library and a few exterior shots. Very, very careful. Nature pictures were easy, and I took several pictures of the town. I even got a picture with a couple moose in the distance. Then I went in the nearest public building and waited until they went away.

But life was certainly not all pictures and moose. I ended up with three major assignments due the same day, which involved some finagling, even with staying on top of things. Only had to pull one all-nighter though.

The Spring Dance was fast approaching, and Allison was once again looking for volunteers to help. While most of us helped her with setting up for the Halloween Dance, we were a little more reluctant this time, simply because there were so many other things we needed to be doing.

"Well, anyone who helps for at least two hours gets a free ticket. And the dance is only a few hours long. So who's in?" Allison smiled at us hopefully.

Without meaning to, I shot a glance at Adrian. He had been my date at the Halloween Dance, but only because Tim and Ilse cajoled him into it. He said he wanted to, and he had fun, but he hadn't said anything about the Spring Dance.

I wasn't sure quite what to think. Did he not want to go? He had been reluctant to go to the Halloween Dance. Maybe he didn't like dances. Maybe he didn't want to go with me. Maybe I should actually ask him, but I probably wasn't going to. I did make Ilse promise to stay out of it, and if she heard of anyone else trying to interfere to ask them to do the same. A date wasn't worth anything if it was forced.

Adrian was keeping his head down, like we wouldn't see him if he was quiet. Interestingly enough, Allison wasn't focusing on him. She hadn't been shy about conscripting his help last time.

Kara broke the silence with a shrug. "I think I'll have a little time. I might be able to get Dras to help." Dras was some boy from her Ultimate Frisbee Deathmatch league who had asked her to the dance. I had only met him twice but I didn't get the feeling either were serious about each other. Dras was an ice sprite, which might actually have been why they talked enough for him to ask her out.

"Do be careful in that regard," Tim said. Then he changed the subject before she could get offended. "I plan to attend the dance with Arie, so it is only fitting I assist in the preparations."

Denise begged off, saying she had class and then a major paper to finish. Ilse couldn't make the volunteer session or the dance itself, but was tightlipped as to why. Something about the vampire council or her family. Or both. Either way, I wasn't getting involved unless asked, and possibly not even then. Krystal and Bria weren't around to ask. "I'm not sure. I do have some more work to do on a few papers." I shrugged. "If I have time…"

Adrian remained quiet. What did that mean

exactly? "Are you planning on going to the dance?" Allison asked me. Probably because everyone else had said. Except Adrian.

"Um, I don't know?" Was I going? I didn't particularly want to go to a dance by myself. The only reason I agreed to go to the Halloween Dance was because Tim asked me. Probably because he felt sorry for me unless he had planned from the beginning to force Adrian into going with me. Kind of doubted that one though.

Tim was eyeing Adrian gravely. While neither of us had actually *said* we were kinda dating, we weren't exactly hiding it either. Had Ilse passed on my message? "Are you going to the dance?" He asked Adrian. Yeah, that was subtle.

"Nope." Adrian didn't even look up.

"I see. And Violet–"

Adrian cut him off. "Can do what she wants. Not your business."

I felt my eyebrows raise. That was snippier than usual even for him. "It may not be Tim's business, but it is mine."

"Like I said. Do what you want. Go. Don't go." He shrugged.

Right, I was trying not to feel a little hurt here. "Did you hate the Halloween Dance that much? I mean, I had fun."

He finally looked up. "Yeah. Me too."

"Then…"

Allison gave an aggrieved sigh and smacked his arm. Hard enough that he winced. "You… *boy*, you. Just say it."

"What?" Adrian gave her a confused look.

"Tell her *why* you aren't going."

"I have a lab. I can't skip it. Even without… everything," *the oath*, "I can't miss that lab."

"Oh! Yeah, no. School comes first. Go do your lab." Okay, so he wasn't avoiding me, or even the dance in general.

He looked a little apologetic. "You really can just do what you want. If someone asks you…"

I refrained from laughing out loud. "I doubt that will happen. Well, I *do* have a lot of work to do. We'll see what happens."

In the end, I decided against going. The Halloween Dance had been fun, but it wasn't something I wanted to do on my own. Half my friends weren't going, and half of the ones who were going were paired up. Staying home and working on my packing seemed like a better idea.

Packing was a pain. I didn't want to take everything back home, especially since I would be back at Wollaston Lake in about six weeks. But there wasn't anywhere to keep it here, since I had to be moved out when the semester ended. I wasn't the only one with that issue. Kara was venting about it two days after the dance. That's when Allison made the suggestion that just might get her nominated for sainthood. "I'm staying over the summer. Well, in and out. Anyway, I'm here enough to keep my room. I don't have a lot of space, but I can store some things for anyone who needs it. Oof!" Kara cut her off with a bear hug.

"You are a treasure, Allison," I said. Hmm, Allison had her room, but Adrian didn't say anything. Maybe he was actually going home for a change. Good. I think. Adrian didn't look up, as he was studiously manipulating a forkful of some meat I didn't recognize around his plate.

"Oh! Roommate assignments have been made, they're supposed to be given out over the next few days." Kara was practically bouncing in her seat. "Yeah, we'll probably get our requests, but it also says what dorm and room we'll be in."

"How do they give them out? I mean, roommate request forms were passed out by the RA, but they were all the same. Do they do the same thing with the assignments?" I asked.

"Unless they changed it, they mail you the results. Well, not exactly mail. It should be in your school mailbox," Allison said.

"Oooh, I know. We shouldn't open the letters until we have them. We can compare notes… next time we meet." Kara looked around to make sure no one was listening.

I couldn't think of a good reason why we'd bother with that. But I couldn't think of a good reason not to, either.

As it happened, we all had our letters within two days. Also as it happened, that was the day the last of us turned in our last final project before exams. So we had a 'legitimate' reason to celebrate before finals began next week.

"Let's open them at the same time," Kara suggested when we met in one of the library study rooms. Again, having no reason not to, we followed her lead.

I ripped open my envelope, expecting to see Ilse was my roommate. Or if not her, then Kara. Instead, I saw this.

Student Name: Violet Peters **Current Roommate:** Ilse Teps **Current Room:** Price Hall 613 **New Roommate Assignment:** Phyna Zaytz **New Room Assignment:** Addams 108

Phyna? Why Phyna? She was the dragon who lived next to Kara and Denise. We weren't close, but we were on friendly terms. I could definitely think of worse candidates. But why? Ilse and I requested each other, and Kara and I requested each other as secondary choices. I didn't know Phyna well, but doubted she would go out of her way to request me.

"Who is Lyta Wrantor?" Ilse asked. "Does anyone

know?"

"Name sounds familiar. I think she's in my Interdimensional Politics class. But I can't place her. Tim, do you know?"

Tim looked up at my question. "Yes, I recall the name. I would not swear to it, but I believe she may be a shadow elemental."

"That would explain why my room assignment is underground." Ilse eyed the paper distastefully. "Though, that is the only matter explained."

"I have another werewolf. Teresa. She's from my hometown." Kara sounded upset about this. That was odd. There were very, very few people Kara did not seem pleased to be around.

"A friend?" Allison asked cautiously.

"No," Kara said shortly and didn't elaborate. No one asked anything else.

"I have Jessica. She's a shifter, like me. Butterfly, I think." Denise was mellower in her reaction, but she was still frowning.

"Krystal and I still have each other." At least one of us got what we wanted.

"And I have Slate." Time sounded relieved.

Adrian shrugged. "Restlo," he said, naming his roommate of the past two years.

"Violet, who do you have?" Allison asked, leaning forward, intent on something.

"Phyna. At least I know her. And she hasn't been anti-human."

"Well, that's something." Kara huffed. "But I don't understand this. Why... we requested each other. Why are we scattered everywhere?"

"If someone trying to close the school is high enough to meddle with room assignments, we have a problem," Adrian, ever the optimist, said.

"Maybe. Or maybe the faculty has noticed a group of students who managed to consistently be in the middle of strange things going down. And maybe they decided that things would be better off if they were split apart." I sighed. It made sense, but I really hated to think about it that way.

"Then why did I keep Bria as my roommate, and Tim and Adrian keep theirs?" Krystal asked.

"You two are twins. They weren't going to be able to separate you anyway, so they might as well keep you together. And neither the yeti's roommate nor mine have been involved in any of our... adventures." What was it with Adrian's reluctance to use people's names?

"I fear you're right." Allison stared off into the distance, not looking at anything. Great, psychic hints. Wonderful. Then she focused back on me. "Violet, I hate to ask, but can I shake your hand?"

Allison's psychic abilities were enhanced greatly by touch. Something she hadn't warned me about before the first time she shook hands with me. I wasn't sure why she was asking now. Perhaps she had picked up on my unease of psychic-ness. It wasn't that I minded that she or Adrian were psychics, I just still had a little trouble with the fact that psychics actually existed.

I stood up so I could reach her. Allison took my hand and her eyes immediately lost focus.

"Beware. Factors are in play. The reluctant enemy and the forced ally will both harm you in the intent to help. You will misplace your trust. The web tightens, and you must out spin the spider. The spider will bite, and you must not fall to the poison." Then she was back. "Owww." She breathed out. "That one really hurt."

We stared at her. Fear was solidifying in my stomach and I didn't think it was all mine. I swallowed hard. "Okay… um. Do you have any good news? How inevitable are your predictions anyway?"

"Indeed," said Ilse. She had pulled out her fortune stones set.

"Not sure about the good news part. As for 'inevitable' well, yes, they will happen. But there is a matter of degree. Something bad *is* going to happen and you *are* going to misplace your trust. But by knowing that ahead of time, you can be careful to hold back your trust as much as possible. Yes, at least one or two people you trust will be the wrong people, but if you don't give *much* trust, hopefully they won't be able to hurt you a lot. That's the best I can tell you. I'm sorry." Allison wouldn't meet my eyes.

"Reluctant enemy and forced ally, that's important. We need to figure out who they are," Adrian spoke up, taking attention away from his sister.

"Definitely. You have to know who you *can* trust, at least the best you can." Kara nodded.

"But she said they would be attempting to *help*," I pointed out. "I think that scares me the most."

"As it likely should," Ilse murmured.

"Reluctant enemy isn't hard to understand," Adrian said. "But a forced ally…"

"Someone who has no choice but to go along with her, or with us in general. But they do not wish to. So why get involved?" Tim mused.

"A great many possibilities. That is the only way a particular goal can be achieved. A personal or family treaty. An…" Ilse trailed off, realizing the same thing we all did.

"An oath." I don't know who said it, I barely heard it. I was too busy sharing horrified looks with the other people in the room as we all realized that the 'forced ally' could be in this room right now.

Chapter Three

Summertime Stress

Somehow I always manage to forget how much traveling from Wollaston Lake, Saskatchewan to Newport News, Virginia wears me out. Ten or more hours of traveling, four airports, three planes, and two time zones. Add that all together, and you get a Violet zombie. The braindead, walking into walls kind. Not the intelligent kind like Dr. Zyloas who works in the school infirmary. She was the only zombie I had seen in Hyde so far, which was fine with me. Dr. Zyloas seemed to be a perfectly intelligent, nice person. I still had a little trouble getting past the zombie part. I'd have to work on it. My Chemistry professor was going to be a zombie.

"Violet, over here!" A voice pulled me from my musings. But not the voice I was expecting.

"Jesse?" I gave him a hug, which he returned with… reluctance? Weird. "I wasn't expecting you."

"Had a free evening and said I'd pick you up. I figured we'd need to talk."

We did. We really truly did. But I wasn't sure I could think clearly right now. "'Kay. Need my luggage first."

Newport News airport is tiny, and I think my flight might have been the only one to have landed recently. So I had my backpack and suitcase quickly. I started to walk away.

"That's it? I thought you took more than that to school."

"Allison is staying the summer, she said we could store some stuff in her room." Since most of what I was leaving was heavy clothes and school books, I was able to fit it all in my duffle bag, which we stored under her bed. I was glad because it meant I wasn't making her already small room smaller.

"Allison… Allison? Did I meet Allison?"

"Pretty sure. Adrian's sister." Judging by Jesse's scowl, he remembered Adrian just fine.

"So, you're still going back."

Why was he surprised by this? "Yes, of course."

"Even though–"

"Jesse, I'm not up for this tonight. I'm exhausted, hungry, and stressed out. I'm going back. Period. If you want to have a *calm, civil* discussion about it, then please remember, I'll be here for weeks. But don't think you'll win. I would really rather not spend the whole summer arguing."

He sighed and loaded my suitcase into his car. Neither of us said a word until we were inside, buckled up, and Jesse started the engine. "I'm just worried about you."

"I know. What did you tell them?"

"The school is intense, more than I was expecting. There was also a much stronger anti-American bias than I expected and we had both run afoul of it a few times. You made friends though, which is why you didn't want to leave. You were busy with classes, school work, and school activities, so we didn't talk a lot, and that's probably why you were so bad at keeping in touch."

Okay, I could work with that. "I took some pictures." Jesse slammed the brakes. "Careful! I took safe pictures. My room, some of my friends, safe parts of buildings, the town, some nature shots."

"Good. That should help. Your mom is worried. We all are, really."

I winced. "I know. Look, I really need your help with this. You know I can't tell them, and you can't either. Please help me reassure them that I'm not crazy or involved in a cult or something?"

"I'm not sure you aren't."

"Jesse!"

"I won't lie to them and I still don't think you should be involved. But I'll try not to blow your cover. I'll do what I can."

"Thanks. I owe you." I breathed a sigh of relief.

"You can leave Hyde." He smiled.

"No."

"Stop hanging out with that group?"

"No!"

"Fine, fine." Jesse mumbled under his breath. "Hey, Violet? Welcome home."

I smiled and thanked him, even as part of me wondered if I really was. Welcome or home.

* * *

No one asked me a single question about Hyde that first night. Considering how disastrous Christmas break was, I wasn't surprised. I didn't want a return to that disaster, and no one else did either. It wouldn't last, I could already feel the simmering tension, but no eruptions that first night.

The next day I enacted my plan. After helping clean up from breakfast, I went upstairs to my computer and printed out a few sheets of pictures. Pictures I had carefully selected and emailed to myself. My camera might be in my bag, but the memory card that held all my school pictures was still at Hyde, under Allison's bed. Mom searched my room last Christmas. I wasn't taking the chance of her or Rose snooping through my pictures.

Everyone was still downstairs. Good. "Hey, I thought you might like to see some pictures of Hyde." I was looking at Mom, but tried to make sure that Rose and Dad knew they were included too. It was the first time anyone mentioned the school since I came back.

"I'd love to." Mom moved some of the brochures

she had been looking at to make room on the table. Soon everyone was gathered around. I put down the stack and started playing figurative tour guide.

"Okay, this is the sitting room of our suite. The computer came with the room. This door is to my room, and that one is to Ilse's. That one's the bathroom."

"How come you rated a suite?" Dad asked. "You're on scholarship, I doubt they paid for fancy room fees."

"Actually, apparently this is standard. I don't know why." Unless Kara was right about it being so people didn't kill each other.

"It's boring looking," Rose said.

I laughed. "I'm told it's nice for a dorm." Mom and Dad murmured agreement. The next picture was the bathroom, which I hadn't thought would need an explanation, but Rose asked me about a big bottle of some sort of gel, whose label wasn't in English. "That's Ilse's. I think it's like a type of soap." Vampires are sensitive to water, so she usually used that to get clean.

Next two pictures were my room, after I made sure it was clean. "This is my room. Not particularly interesting, but it was nice enough. Well, it was my room." The bed was made and the purple teddy bear Rose gave me for my birthday was next to my old teddy bear, Mendel. My desk showed signs of frequent use, with the books carefully stacked so the spines weren't visible.

"I didn't take a picture of Ilse's room, since that

wasn't any of my business, but here is Ilse." I pointed to a picture. Ilse had deliberately chosen her least formal clothes for this shot. She still looked like a model.

"She's gorgeous!" Rose exclaimed. "Is she rich? She looks rich."

"Rose! That isn't any of our business," Mom scolded.

"I never asked her about money, but her parents are involved in the government of her home country. Apparently fairly influential." I let them draw their own conclusions from that. "She's really nice though. A little formal, since she's used to dealing with politicians all the time; but she never looked down on me or anyone else for not being as rich or influential as she was. She helped me learn a lot."

"Well, that's good. She's awfully pale," Dad noted.

"Wollaston Lake is near the arctic circle. The lake is still frozen. There aren't a whole lot of opportunities for tanning." I was looking pretty pale myself, which helped back up my story.

"True. So why is someone so… upper-class attending a dinky little school there?" Dad asked.

"Family tradition. Besides, I think she wanted to be 'normal' for a little while. Her brother went to Hyde. I haven't met him, he graduated a few years ago." Ten years to be precise. I moved on to the next picture.

"Okay, this is what the floor of the dorm looks like." It was tricky getting a shot where no one was in the hallway. Took me at least five tries. "I'm on the end. And across from me is Kara and Denise. This is their sitting room." Even in a still picture you could tell Kara was waving enthusiastically while Denise just gave a small smile. I pointed to each as I continued. "Kara is Canadian, from the Yukon region." Apparently in a town that was in her dimension as well as mine. "Denise is from the Bahamas. We complain about how cold it is there." Actually, Denise didn't complain a lot.

"Here is the floor lounge." I pointed out the various people sitting there, homework scattered across the table. "That's Sylvia, this is Cal, and over in that corner is Felicity. I don't know any of them that well, I'm afraid."

The next picture was the outside of the hall. Then the outside of the library. The pictures inside the library were, deliberately, not clear enough to pick up the titles of the books. Bria posed for me in one of the library study rooms, allowing me to explain those. I did mention that they were available for students, could be reserved, and were quiet. I did not mention they were magically soundproofed, and the privacy measures were magic based too. Despite my worries, Bria's blue tinted hair didn't get a single remark.

"This is one of the rooms in the gym. Students practice aerobics and other stuff here. Adrian, here," I ignored the frowns, "has been teaching some of us a bit about stick fighting."

"Why?" Mom asked.

I shrugged. "Some of it for the exercise, some of it for 'just in case'." That was close enough, right? I pointed to a picture of him sparring with Allison. "That's his sister, Allison. She's on the alumni association, so she's always back and forth at the college."

Before they could ask more about that, I moved on. "This is Professor Collins. She teaches Practical Life Applications." That was what the transcript called it. Probably because 'Magic for Non-Magic Users' would cause a bit of a fuss some places. "I wasn't able to get pictures of any of my other teachers, sorry."

Most of the rest of the shots were either nature shots or pictures of the town. I filled in a bit about that, telling about the friendly general store manager/post man who had been kind enough to give me a ride to the ferry when I arrived with luggage and made a point of greeting me when I went to town. There were a couple pictures of Adrian making balloon animals and putting on a show with them for the kids. I reassured Mom that no, I did not get anywhere close to the moose, that was with zoom. Yes, I did go inside afterwards. No, moose never came as far as the school.

"You didn't take any pictures of the ferry," Rose complained. "You said that was pretty. I wanted to see it."

"Sorry, the ferry is out of commission until the ice melts. That's usually in June." Rose shivered. "Yeah, gets fun."

"Did you take pictures of all your friends?" Mom asked. "You mentioned something about a young man inviting a group of you somewhere?"

"Tim. He's… well, a little camera shy. He didn't want his picture taken." I hadn't even asked him. Hard to pass off an eight foot tall yeti as anything other than a yeti. Or maybe an albino Bigfoot. But I wasn't completely lying. He didn't seem to enjoy being in pictures, even joining group shots reluctantly. "Tim is nice. You'd like him." If she got past the 'yeti' part. "Very polite, smart. He's a Lit major. Anyway, his parents were going to be close by, at a tourist attraction, forget the name, so he invited us all to visit. It was a lot of fun." I couldn't pronounce the name of the town the North Pole was located in in his dimension. That counted as forgetting, right?

"And everyone went?" Mom asked.

"Ilse, Kara and Denise, Krystal and Bria; Krystal is Bria's twin sister. Um, Adrian and Allison; Arie, I didn't get any pictures of her, and Tim's roommate. I shared a room with Ilse, Arie, and Allison." I smiled. "Which meant I was the only one whose name didn't start with a vowel."

Rose snickered at that. "Why didn't you take a picture of Arie?"

"Arie… well, we're not really friends, so much as we're both Tim's friend. We aren't enemies or anything, but we aren't on wonderful terms. I didn't want to ask her for a picture." All of which was true, and ignored the fact that she was a harpy and I wouldn't be able to show them pictures of her anyway.

"Did you get any pictures of your trip?" Dad asked.

Should have known they'd ask that. "Yeah, but they didn't turn out too great. I don't have them here." That was mostly true, it was too dark to take decent pictures with my cheap camera.

"What was your favorite class?" Mom asked, when she saw that I was done showing pictures.

"Basics of Genetics. Without a doubt. I like the teacher, I've had him for two other classes, and I managed to sign up for his zoology class next semester. He was also my Bio II teacher, which was great. Practical Life Applications was also a lot of fun. Professor Collins has an amazing sense of humor, was always tossing out zingers to keep us on our toes."

"What about least favorite?" Dad asked.

"Probably Government. Tim and Arie were in that class with me, so was Jesse when he was there. That was okay, but a lot of the material was new, and everyone had to do at least one public debate. I also had Calculus, which was okay." The most interesting thing about Calculus was that the teacher was a tree, and we couldn't use paper at all for that class. "Anyway, I've now fulfilled my math requirements. Next semester, I have Zoology, Botany, another history class, another music class, and Chem II. Bio majors need to have some Chem classes. Adrian's a Chemistry major, so he advised me on which professors to take." I would be taking Chem I during the summer intensive, July to Mid-August. But I had told them that already.

"Why music?" Dad asked.

"I needed another Fine Arts class, and I liked Professor Shale." I had made a point of asking her if she minded me taking another class with her because she had been so uncomfortable with me after the incident in the library. Maybe time and distance had helped, or maybe she was embarrassed that I basically asked her permission. Either way, she agreed. Next semester, I was taking Interdimensional Classics. "Anyway, I'm almost done with my required classes, and I really need to pick a minor soon." Hyde certainly had some interesting options, only about half of which I could tell my family about.

I didn't have all my grades yet, but the ones I did have were good. More importantly, I seemed to have reassured my family. With luck, I would avoid the problems of last Christmas.

I hoped so. The last couple weeks of school had been tense enough. No one wanted to think it, but once the thought occurred that the 'forced ally' might be part of the oath group, I couldn't let go of it. Neither could anyone else. It was agony to think about, that one of 'our group' might not want to be there, and could betray… me? Us? The group? I didn't even know. Whichever, the thought caused physical pain, in my breastbone and throat. So I tried not to think about it. But I couldn't. It was like messing with a bruise. I had to keep poking it to see if it would still hurt.

Unfortunately, even if the person wasn't in the oath group, if Allison was right, I was going to be betrayed. By someone who thought they were helping me. Fun. But I couldn't see how withdrawing from my friends would help anything. We'd be keeping in touch over the summer, like we did over Christmas break. Mostly by email, since we could use the school accounts. That was the easiest way around interdimensional communication.

My pre-emptive strike of sharing about the school seemed to help a lot. I still got asked questions I wasn't sure how to answer, but not as many. No one wanted another fight. Having shown them pictures of the school and my friends apparently reassured my parents I hadn't joined a cult or something. Neither Mom nor I mentioned her searching my room at Christmas, the final straw that sent me back to school early. Whatever the reason, the next few days were calm.

I visited Linda Green, my high school biology teacher, a couple times. She was an alumna of Hyde, and one of the reasons Hyde became my dream school. I don't think Mom liked her much, both because it was her suggestion that had me breeding fruit flies for several months in high school, and because over Christmas, I would avoid home to talk to her because I didn't have to keep secrets from her. I didn't hide the fact I was visiting her, but I didn't rub it in either.

I needed those visits. There weren't the same angry undercurrents as Christmas break, but there was still the feeling of walking tiptoes on eggshells and bubbles over a pit of broken glass. Or maybe that was just me. It was nice to talk to someone who understood.

What surprised me was Jesse. I should have been able to talk to him. Not only had he been at Hyde, granted for barely a month, but he had been there at the same time I was and knew many of the same people. He should have been a great person to talk to. But Jesse was acting weird. Withdrawn, quiet, if I didn't know better I'd say he was avoiding me.

"Yeah, he's been like that since he changed schools," Rose said when I asked her about it. "He doesn't like talking about it."

The same way I had been when I came back for Christmas. No wonder everyone was so nervous. "Does he seem to like his new school?"

Rose rolled her eyes, and tried to snitch a cookie off my plate, pouting as I moved the plate further away. "I'll say. It's about the only thing that he gets excited about anymore." She frowned. "I don't like your school."

I couldn't blame her for that, and wasn't sure what to say. Instead, I gave her a sideways hug, ignoring when she took advantage of it to steal the cookie. "It's not the school's fault. Not really." More like the people involved with the school. "It's just… different. Jesse had a harder time adjusting. Don't worry, you'll get the old Jesse back." I hoped.

"What about you? Will I get the old you back?" Rose stared at the table as if it held the answers to the mysteries of the universe and next week's math test.

I hugged her harder. How could I tell her that Violet was gone for good? She died the night her roommate said she was a vampire.

***

It took nearly a week before I had a good chance to talk to Jesse alone. Even then, it was more a coincidence than a plan. Leaving Linda Green's house, I spotted Jesse, probably walking back from the library. He waited when I called out to him, and let me catch up. When I did, I wasn't sure what to say. I had been out of it when he picked me up at the airport, and might not have noticed if the sky had turned orange. But now I could clearly see that Jesse looked worn. Thinner, maybe a little haggard. Like he hadn't been sleeping.

"Are you okay?" It was a dumb thing to ask.

"Fine." That was an even dumber answer.

"You don't look fine."

"And you continue going to a school that puts you in danger. You don't seem to want *my* concern."

I physically flinched at that. "Sorry."

That seemed to deflate his ire. "Yeah, me too. Haven't slept well recently. Dead week, you know."

"Oh, I remember." Personally, I hated that more than the week of finals that came after. That probably wasn't the only reason he looked horrible though. "Well, I hope you get some sleep soon."

We were drifting somewhat aimlessly in the vague direction of his house. I kept an eye out for anyone listening, watching, or following us. Jesse noticed.

"Paranoid much?"

"Habit. Useful habit."

He shook his head. "You have to get out of that school." With a sudden step, he was in front of me, and grabbed my shoulders. "No, I mean it. It's dangerous and pulls you away from everything. Do you know how much trouble I've had adjusting, and I was only gone a month! I can barely talk to anyone, I'm driving myself crazy wondering what is real. Can't remember the last time I slept through the night. It's killing me, Violet. I wish I had never even heard of Hyde! I wish you hadn't either." Jesse stopped, perhaps realizing he was shaking me. He let go.

"Jesse..." What could I tell him? It would get better? I didn't know that. I couldn't go back to who I was before, not for anything. I couldn't even wish I'd never gone to Hyde. Though I did wish he hadn't gone. "I'm sorry."

"Not your fault. I know that. Maybe this is easier for you than me. I sure hope so. But I kind of don't."

"So I'd give up and come home?" No way was I telling him I had made an oath swearing to do my best to keep the school open. That meant sticking around, even at risk to myself.

"Just..." He rubbed at his face, then squinted at something across the street. "Hey, is that Adrian?"

Chapter Four

Dinner Détente

I followed Jesse's gaze even while part of me was thinking, 'No, it couldn't possibly be Adrian because Adrian is in Canada.' But even as I was about to say something to that effect, I spotted him. Sure enough, Adrian was across the street. Looking disgruntled at being spotted.

We crossed the street, Jesse reaching him before I did. "What? It wasn't enough for you to stalk my cousin at school, you had to follow her here too?"

"Jesse! Adrian, what are you doing here? I thought you were going home."

Scarily enough, Adrian looked even worse than Jesse. He rubbed a hand over his face. "I did. It... didn't work."

I winced. "Sorry." Not even a week. Yikes!

"Don't your parents know about... everything?" Jesse asked.

"Yes. It doesn't help as much as you'd think."

"That still doesn't explain what you're doing here. This isn't that stupid school of yours. You have no reason to stalk Violet here, and you had certainly better not be expecting her family to put you up while you avoid your own family."

Adrian drew back, there was a growl reverberating under his voice. "In reverse order, that would be rude and presumptuous. I reserved a hotel room. I am not stalking Violet, and it is certainly possible for her to be in danger even here. Less likely, but certainly possible."

"Food poisoning," I muttered under my breath.

Jesse didn't hear me. That was fine, it wasn't for him. Adrian did hear me, and even better, he started to calm down.

"She wouldn't be in any danger at all if it wasn't for that school."

"Quite possible. But she did go. Too late for looking back."

Jesse's cellphone rang, almost making me jump. Cellphones don't work at Hyde, so I had given mine to Rose. Honestly, I had forgotten Jesse had one.

"Hello? Oh, hi. Yes, Violet's with me. We ran into one of her friends from school. Apparently Adrian is visiting. No, she didn't know. Yeah, sure, you can talk to her." He smirked at my wide-eyed look. "It's your mom."

With great reluctance and trepidation, I took the phone. "Hi, Mom? Yeah, I'm fine. Yes. Yes. Right, okay. Be back soon." I'm sure my smile was a bit sickly as I hung up and turned to Adrian. "You're invited over for dinner."

***

Dinner was the most awkward meal I had ever experienced. Ever. That included sharing a table with Tim and Arie. That included breakfast right before I left for school early during Christmas break. It even included the dinner after I had accidentally set significant portions of the kitchen on fire when I was twelve. I was never allowed to use my chemistry set unsupervised again.

Anyway, this dinner left them all in the dust. It was like this meal was aiming for the Awkward Meals Hall of Fame. I really hope there isn't such a thing.

Maybe it wouldn't have been quite so bad if Jesse hadn't stayed over too. Then again, I'm not sure his not being there would have helped. Actually, I'm not sure anything would have helped.

"So, Adrian, right? Violet's told us a lot about you. Why did you choose to come to Newport News?" Mom asked.

I honestly did not know how Adrian was going to answer that. I wasn't sure how he *could* without sounding like a creepy stalker or insanely paranoid. "Part of it was to visit Violet, of course. But she's also told me about interesting places in the area." I had what? "She mentioned areas like Colonial Williamsburg, Jamestown, Yorktown, and others that have such history." Yes, I had mentioned those. A couple times. I hadn't realized he was interested. "She also mentioned how she sometimes missed the ocean. I'm from Toronto, I've never actually seen the ocean. I figured why not, and if I'm going to see it, why not be far enough south to enjoy it?"

Wow, smooth, Adrian. I wondered how much of

it was true. But it sounded somewhat reasonable.

"How long were you planning on staying?" Dad asked.

"I'm due to go back for the second summer intensive, but I probably won't stay *here* the whole time. After all, it's a new country and a big one at that."

"Did you really stalk my sister?"

I winced at Rose's blunt question. Adrian was fighting a flinch too. "I suppose it could be called that. Not my finest moment, and I'm not proud of it. I also apologize if I made her or any of you uncomfortable. Just remember, boys get stupid when hormones are involved," He half-whispered to Rose, making her giggle.

"That doesn't mean stalking is appropriate," Jesse muttered.

"No, it really isn't. Violet pointed that out when we moved to actually talking to each other. I... should have handled things differently. All I can say is that it seemed a good idea at the time."

Dad laughed. "I can understand that, a bit. But you don't think so now, right?" Adrian shook his head. "Good. So, tell us about your family. You have a sister?" Oh, great.

"Allison. She majored in Psychology, and is on the Hyde Alumni committee. Means she's going back and forth to the school a lot. She's awesome, and probably the main reason I have any friends on campus."

"What about your parents?" Mom asked. "Aren't they a bit worried about you roaming a strange country?"

"No, not really." That dripped in bitterness. Adrian seemed to realize it and tried to cover. "It's a little complicated. But distance doesn't bother them. Or me."

"Are you going to marry Violet?" Rose asked.

Adrian choked on his water. I dropped my fork. Mom and Dad looked scandalized. Jesse looked angry. "Rose!" I choke-shrieked.

"Um, not this summer. Promise."

"Who's up for dessert?" I ignored the fact that most of us weren't done eating. "Adrian brought over a cake. It looks great."

Mom helped me dish up the cake. I guess she wanted to change the subject too. The cake was chocolate, with white chocolate frosting. It was delicious and I would have to ask Adrian how he found a bakery this good, this quickly.

The interrogation continued, but it was a little lower key. When he mentioned he was a Chemistry major, Rose took advantage of that to tell him the story of the time I set fire to the kitchen with my chemistry set. I don't think I've ever seen Adrian laugh that hard. Or Jesse, for that matter. It eased some of my resentment, if not my embarrassment. He was asked about future plans. Mom asked about the anti-American sentiment.

Good thing Adrian caught on quick. "It isn't

actually that large or popular a view, but they are, well, vocal. Most don't care, and some are fascinated by it. I think Violet might be the only American at the moment, so she gets all the fallout." Dad expressed surprise and disbelief that I could be the *only* American. "Small school, in the middle of nowhere. Most students are legacy students. Their parents went, maybe siblings." He shrugged.

"But you do have international students. Violet mentioned that her one friend is from Europe and another from the Bahamas," Dad pointed out.

"Some international, but mostly part of the former or current British Empire. Like Canada." Adrian shrugged again. "Don't know why the American specific bias."

"Do you speak French?" Rose asked.

"*Mais oui, Mademoiselle.*" Adrian gave a seated half bow. "I'm semi-bilingual. Most Canadians are. Not everyone, of course. But schools teach both, and most official notices are in both English and French."

"Then why only semi-bilingual?" Jesse asked.

"My vocabulary is about intermediate level. I don't know technical terms, most advanced vocabulary, and could get lost if the conversation goes too fast." Or at least, he would if it wasn't for the translation spell.

"It's still loads better than my French," I said. "I don't get to practice it much." The same spell meant I didn't always notice when I was exposed to a foreign language. Certainly didn't help me learn one.

"Is English your first language, or is French?" Rose asked.

"I was exposed to both from birth, but we primarily spoke English in my house and neighborhood."

Dessert was finished and Adrian started making excuses to get back to his hotel. When he mentioned which one, I recognized it as one close-by, and offered to walk with him. Jesse immediately said he'd drive us over. Before either Adrian or I could say anything, Mom agreed.

"I don't need a chaperone," I said as I climbed in the front seat. Normally I would have offered it to Adrian, but I thought it best to keep them as separate as possible.

"You thought you could walk a strange boy to a hotel and not have your parents object?"

"He's not wrong." Adrian's backing Jesse up surprised us both. "Appearances matter to some."

The drive wasn't long, and Jesse did wait in the car while I walked Adrian up to the door. This gave me a small chance to ask what I couldn't ask in front of my family, even Jesse.

"Do you think I'm in danger? Is that why you came?"

"Not immediate danger. Honestly, I wasn't sure

where else to go."

What did one even say to that? "Well, I don't mind the visit."

Adrian smiled, a small, crooked smile. "Good. Um, here. It's the number to the phone in my hotel room."

"Oh, thanks. I don't have a private phone line, but here." I scribbled down the number on a piece of junk paper I had stuffed in my pocket. "This is the home phone. But be aware that someone else might answer. Or listen in. Email is more secure. Um, sorry about the interrogation. And Rose…"

"It's fine. Trust me, I tormented Allison's friends a few times myself."

I snickered, trying to picture Adrian as a bratty teenager, annoying his sister and her friends. It wasn't too hard. "Is that why she's always teasing you now? Payback?"

"No, she did that then too."

That won a full laugh from me. And an impatient honk of the horn from Jesse. "My ride's waiting."

"Yeah." Adrian smirked. "If I kissed you now…"

He had kissed me at New Year's, but not really since. I wasn't sure quite how I felt about that. Judging from how hot my face felt, I must have been blushing hard. "I think he'd climb out of the car to murder you."

"He could try."

"We could not torture him. Yet. Wait until he deserves it. Goodnight, Adrian."

"Goodnight, Violet." He took my hand and kissed it. Tim did that sometimes, but Adrian generally only did that kind of thing when he was showing off his manners.

I did the best I could at a curtsey while wearing jeans before turning back to the car. When I looked back, Adrian had opened his door, but was watching me to make sure I made it safely to the car.

The ride back home was silent. Jesse managed to exude disapproval and moodiness so much that even when I had my back to him and stared out the window, I could feel it. He dropped me off at home, but didn't stop in. "Thanks for the ride." It was the first thing either of us had said since dropping off Adrian.

He didn't acknowledge me as he pulled away. Shaking my head, I went inside. Mom and Dad were in the living room. Rose was nowhere to be seen. "Did Rose go to bed?"

"Something like that," Mom said.

"It's barely nine o'clock." I looked at my watch. Yup, nine-ten. "Why so early?"

"Sit down, Violet," Dad said.

Oh, that was why. Great. I sat down. "Yes?"

"Did you know that boy would be coming here?" Dad asked.

I frowned. Jesse had told them I didn't. Maybe they wanted confirmation. "It was a complete surprise to me."

Oddly, that made them more upset. "So he never mentioned anything about possibly visiting this country over the summer?" Mom asked.

"Nothing. I thought he would be with his family. Or maybe the school."

"Why *isn't* he with his family?" Mom asked. "A boy his age shouldn't be wandering around strange countries alone."

"He said he did visit his family. Since he left school when I did, I decided not to ask any questions. He… doesn't seem close to his parents."

"I noticed," Dad muttered. "Why?"

I shrugged. "He doesn't talk about it, and I didn't think it was my business to ask. In his defense, it seems to be at least as much his parents' fault as his."

Mom started to say something, but Dad put a hand on her knee and she quieted. "What makes you say that?" He asked.

Okay, how did I say this? "Adrian had some trouble last year, even ending up in the infirmary for a couple days. I know Allison called their parents from the start. But they never came, or called, or anything. Allison had to take charge of everything."

"How did he get hurt?" Mom asked.

Oh, someone tried to kill him using magic that the infirmary still hadn't fully deciphered. "Um, snow mobile accident." The instant I said the last word, I knew it was the wrong thing to say. I was never good at lying and tried very hard to avoid it. Hedging the truth, claiming something similar, I had to do that a lot lately. Out and out lying? Really wasn't comfortable with it. Or good at it.

Which is why I wasn't surprised that my parents knew right away that I was lying. "What really happened?" Mom asked. "Why would you cover it up?"

"I…" There was no right answer. I couldn't tell them the truth, they would see through a lie.

"Was he on drugs?" Dad asked.

"What? No! It wasn't his fault at all!"

"Then what did happen?" Mom asked. "Do not lie to us."

"He… kinda got jumped. Almost died." Mom gasped. "He's okay now! And they caught the culprit."

"Why didn't you just say so the first time?" Dad asked.

Before I could try to answer that, Mom cut in.

"Did it happen at the school? Were you there?"

"Yes, it was on campus; no, I wasn't near there."

"Why was he jumped?" Dad asked. "You said there was an anti-American bias. Was he attacked because he is around you a lot?"

"No, not exactly. Actually, it seemed to be more related to something that happened the year before. I don't know all the details."

My parents looked at each other and came to a decision. Before they said anything, I knew I wasn't going to like this. I was right.

"Violet, honey," Mom started. Oh, this was going to be bad. "We don't think you should hang out with this Adrian anymore."

"What?" I couldn't be hearing this correctly.

"He stalked you. He followed you into a *different country* without warning, apparently on impulse, after a fight with his parents. He got involved in some kind of fight that put him in the hospital for days, and you felt the need to lie to us about it. This is not a good influence or a safe person for you to associate with." Dad ticked off each point on his fingers. "Honestly, my first inclination is to drive you to the police station to get a restraining order. Why isn't your school doing something?"

"But... It's not like that! At all."

"You're in too deep to see the situation clearly. In

time, you'll thank us." Mom's voice droned in my ears. I could barely hear it, everything was like static.

"I'll call the school tomorrow, see if they can't do something about him," Dad said.

"No! There's nothing for the school to do. He isn't doing anything wrong!" I wasn't sure if Adrian was still on disciplinary probation or not. Either way, a complaint like that might be enough to get him expelled.

"Violet, we just want what's best for you," Mom said.

"This isn't it!" What could I do? How could I convince them? "Look, I know he can come off looking… odd. But he's a good guy when you get to know him, honestly. He's helped me out a lot."

"According to Jesse, he's manipulated you into thinking you need him," Dad said.

I was going to kill my cousin. Ouch, sudden headache. How much was because of this fight, and how much was because of my sudden murderous thoughts about my cousin? Okay, not kill him, I was going to… Worse headache. "Jesse and Adrian didn't get along from the beginning. I think it's some kind of guy thing. I don't even ask. Adrian has not manipulated me."

Less than surprisingly, they didn't take my word for it that I wasn't being manipulated or misled.

"Would you know if you were?" Mom asked.

"How can I possibly convince you? How can I show you that it isn't what you think?"

"You can start by explaining what *it* is, what you are hiding, and why you are hanging out with him when you know you should be running the other way," Mom said.

"He's my friend. I met him the first day I was at school, he was actually one of the first people I talked to. On the second day, he caught me, preventing me from a nasty fall down the stairs, then I kept seeing him. Becoming friends was a slow process, but we did. He's not very popular. I admit he has poor social skills, and he'd be the first to agree. But he's nice. I showed you the pictures of him entertaining the kids in town, he does that every week, weather permitting. He may not volunteer, but he helps people out without being asked. He just… isn't always good with people."

This wasn't working, I could tell. "Violet–"

I cut Mom off. "Look, you always say we need to be polite, and not necessarily judge by first impressions, right? You don't know him yet."

"That only counts when you aren't putting yourself in danger," Dad said.

"I agree. But if Adrian wanted me hurt, he's had opportunities. He's even stopped me from getting hurt on a couple occasions. Can you at least give him a chance? It's not like he's going to follow me to Newport News, let all my family know he's here, and then try to hurt me, right?"

Mom and Dad managed to have an entire conversation without words. Mom was the one to translate. "Okay, I still don't like him, or trust him; but we will give him a chance. In exchange, we want you to be open to the possibility that he *might* be leading you astray, and take a few precautions. We don't want you alone with him unless you are in a public place. No going to his hotel. No inviting him over if neither your father nor I are home. If he says or does something that makes you uncomfortable, say something. If he doesn't listen, then tell us. And, Violet, if at any time you realize we're right? Say something. We'll help you get away from him. No 'I told you so's, we promise."

"Okay, I can agree to that. Oh, I gave him our phone number."

"Not a problem. But do remember that one of us might end up picking up instead," Dad said.

I nodded. Wow, I felt drained. "Can I go to bed? I'm just... really tired."

"That's fine. Goodnight. Remember, we love you," Mom said.

"I love you too. Goodnight."

Despite my exhaustion I wrote a couple emails first. One to Adrian, to warn him about the conversation with my parents. One to Allison, making sure she knew where her brother was. Maybe she would have some ideas on how to convince my parents everything was okay. I certainly didn't. I considered doing a general email to the group, but I figured I should ask Adrian if he minded first. There was one other person I wanted to talk to, but that would have to wait.

***

Mornings are supposed to begin at noon. That was a long and deeply held belief of mine. As far as I'm concerned, the only reason more people don't realize that is because of a conspiracy by evil morning people. Now, I know not all morning people are evil. Only the ones that force the rest of us to live by their warped and twisted schedule.

I am not a morning person. At all. Not as bad as Allison, who, the one time I tried to wake her up, threw things at me before burrowing under her blankets; but it is rare for me to see a sunrise. Sometimes at Hyde, where the sun rises very late in the winter, but Newport News in summer is a different story.

So I was a little miffed to be standing outside, watching an admittedly exquisite sunrise, waiting. I was tired, stressed, and irritated. Which meant I was in lousy shape for a potentially, or almost certainly, difficult conversation. But it was also my best chance.

It was six-forty-five when Jesse left his house for his daily six-thirty jog. Since I disliked jogging almost as much as I disliked mornings, Jesse could be forgiven his surprise at seeing me there.

"Violet? Are you okay? What's wrong?"

"You're going jogging, right? I want to come too."

He stared at me a few moments, probably noticing I was wearing my practice uniform from lacrosse. But I was determined not to get in a fight right off the bat. No, a little jogging should loosen me up, maybe let me talk to him without screaming and proving him right about my supposed emotional and maybe mental instability.

"Um, okay? Did you take up jogging?"

I shrugged. "Kinda sorta. More walking, but I jog too."

"Sure, right. Two miles good?"

"Don't you usually do five?"

"*Can* you do five?" Jesse asked with great skepticism. "You're more of a sprinter."

"True, probably not five. But I can do three."

"Right. Tell me if I'm going too fast." He did a little warm-up stretching, lifting his eyebrows when I didn't join in. "You're going to get sore."

"I was waiting for you. I'm already warmed up."

"Sorry, wasn't expecting company."

I let Jesse lead and set the pace. He had his own jogging routes, which was more than I had. His pace was slow to start with, but gradually got faster. After a mile, we slowed and did some more stretching. "So, what's with the newfound love of jogging?"

"Staying in shape is important. Very helpful, too."

Plus, it was part of keeping our oath. But Jesse didn't know about the oath. "Besides, I wanted to talk to you."

Jesse sighed and started jogging again. "I was afraid of that."

"Well, then maybe you should have thought about that before you told my parents that Adrian is manipulating me."

"He is."

"A, no, he isn't. B, if you think I'm being manipulated, you tell *me*. Haven't you learned that I react very badly to you going behind my back to convince my parents the situation is worse than it is? That seems very *manipulative*." I stopped to let a black car with a cracked side mirror drive past. Then I followed Jesse across the street.

"First of all, from how I see it, he is. Second, I am so definitely underplaying the situation, *at your insistence*. Third, if I see you are in danger, I'm going to do everything in my power to get you out. If you won't listen, then I'll find someone who will."

The calmer, more rational, part of me could see Jesse's point and was even a little grateful he cared that much. Most of me, on the other hand, was angry and frustrated that he wouldn't listen, wouldn't believe me, and insisted on going behind my back. Unfortunately, I wasn't sure how to convince him to drop it, and let me handle things. "I know what I'm doing, Jesse. I know you don't understand, but part of that is because you left! I don't blame you for leaving, but can you understand that

I have reasons for staying?"

"Is Adrian a reason?"

"No. I'd be at school with or without him. But him being around makes me safer."

Jesse growled and sped up. I followed. We had told Jesse that Adrian was a defender psychic and he had even seen some evidence of it, but Jesse didn't seem to believe it. Or maybe didn't want to believe it. "I still don't like him."

"There's a newsflash. He doesn't seem ready to join your fan club either. On the other hand, he's not going around spreading rumors about you."

"No, he just attacked me when I wasn't looking."

I winced. Yeah, I remembered that, really well. "He said he apologized for that."

Jesse scoffed. "Yeah, he apologized. So I should just forgive and forget that he tried to kill me."

"He didn't try to kill you. In fact, he probably took precautions to make sure you didn't get hurt. Besides, you did try to hit him first."

"What do you mean, 'took precautions'?"

"Do you know how heavy a jaguar is?"

Jesse dodged an exposed tree root. I followed. "No."

"About four hundred pounds. They also have the strongest bite of any cat, second strongest of any land mammal. They bite through turtle shells. You weren't bitten, scratched, or even badly bruised."

"Why are you siding with him?"

"About that fight? I'm not. You were both idiots, and I consider myself fully justified in yelling at the two of you. I was furious with him, but I wasn't exactly proud of you either. Did he start any other fights with you?"

"No," Jesse ground out reluctantly. "But–"

"Let's go home."

"We haven't finished our jog."

"And that's the third time I've seen that car with the cracked side mirror."

Jesse looked at the black car. "Could be a local."

"Could be. Let's go home."

"Yeah. Let's."

Chapter Five

Conversations and Confrontations

I managed to persuade Jesse to keep quiet about the car, but only because he thought I was being paranoid. He seemed to have this impression that Hyde was dangerous and Newport News was 'safe'. He also agreed, once I mentioned my parents' rules about Adrian, not to go causing trouble in that area.

Mom was in the kitchen when I came home, and she was shocked to see me. "You're awake? I thought you were sleeping." She looked me over. "Where were you?"

"Oh, I went jogging with Jesse. Kind of got in the habit of regular exercise at school, and it's much easier to exercise with someone else." All true.

Mom smiled. "Yes it is. Are you going to do this every morning?"

I shrugged. "We'll see." Despite the disagreement, Jesse said it was okay if I joined him in the future. It wasn't like we had to actually talk to each other. Now if only it weren't for the morning part. "Need help with breakfast?"

"Actually, yes. I've got a showing today and need to get changed. Can you finish the bacon?"

"Sure, no problem." I half-saluted her with the spatula and went about stirring up the bacon.

Rose stumbled down a minute later. "Bacon?"

"Ready in a few minutes."

She nodded. "Juice?"

"On the table."

Another nod. Rose poured herself a half glass of pineapple juice, slumped at the table and drank it. Then she looked at me and blinked. "Oh, you aren't Mom."

I laughed. "No. No, I'm not. Were you expecting me to be?"

"Kind of. Why are you making breakfast?"

"Mom's getting changed. She's showing a house today."

"Right. Hey, is your friend coming over today?"

"I don't know. I haven't talked to him about it."

"He's cute."

I bit my lip, trying not to laugh. "Shall I tell him you said so?"

"No!"

I couldn't hold back my laughter anymore. "Okay, I won't tell him."

"Do you think he's cute?"

Okay, there was a bit of a blush. I turned back to the stove. "How crispy do you want your bacon?"

"You're changing the subject."

"If I told you I thought him cute, or hot, or mildly attractive, or anything of the sort, you'd tell him. With glee."

"Well, yeah. But do you?"

"You never answered about the bacon."

"You haven't said no. So it's yes. You think he's cute. You like him. Violet and Adrian sitting in a–"

"Rose!"

Dad walked in then. "What's going on in here?"

"Nothing!" We said in unison, trying to look innocent. I don't think it worked. I also think Dad decided he didn't want to know.

"Right. Where's your mother?"

Mom came down then, wearing her pink blazer and pearls. "Breakfast ready yet?"

Breakfast went pretty well. Adrian wasn't mentioned once after I said I didn't know if I would see him today. Rose chortled at that, but didn't say anything. It was Rose's turn to do dishes, so I took the chance to slip away and check my email.

Both Char siblings had written back. I checked

Adrian's first. He said he understood completely and agreed to the restrictions, then asked if I wanted to meet him for lunch at a local café. That made me think. Mom was showing a house. Dad didn't have work until Monday. No one had mentioned plans. I gave him a tentative yes, to be changed if something came up.

Allison's reply was even better. She was pleased to know where Adrian was, since she had been worried when he disappeared. If she could arrange it in her schedule, she might pop down for a couple days. Perhaps meeting her would help reassure my parents. But she also suggested having my parents talk to Taria.

Taria was probably the most important person on campus. She wasn't the Dean, but she had been part of the school since it was founded. To the best of anyone's knowledge, there was no other of her kind; just her, the immortal purple telepathic winged shapeshifter. Hyde was her baby. She was also the student advisor to every human who had gone to Hyde in the past hundred years. I don't know if she was Adrian's advisor too, but she certainly knew him, and his circumstances.

Honestly, I wasn't so sure about that idea. It wasn't that I didn't like or trust Taria, but I wasn't used to going to teachers over personal issues. Besides, Taria had made it clear that while yes, things were happening behind the scenes at the school, we were to let the faculty handle it. We had pretty much ignored that part.

But Allison said that Taria would be expecting my call and left a number. I re-read that part of the email.

I wouldn't have told her, but she is my boss and

*was nearby when I read your email. She said you should
probably talk to her first, so you can get your stories
straight. She also says that this isn't the first time she's
had to reassure parents that everything is fine, and no,
their child is not going crazy.*

It was a little reassuring to know that I wasn't the
only one to have this problem. According to my clock it
wasn't even eight here, and it was two hours earlier at
Hyde. Probably too early to call now. Maybe after lunch.

***

I met Adrian at the diner he had suggested. It was
one I hadn't been to before, despite being a native of the
area. Not sure I would have tried it if he hadn't suggested
it. Maybe Adrian had a soft spot for diners. Adrian was
already sitting in the back. "Hey, am I late?"

"No. You're fine." He stood and pulled out my
seat.

"Thanks. How did you do on your math test?"

Adrian chuckled, but went with it. "Not too bad.
Hope to do better on the next. You should have checked
yesterday."

"Yeah, probably should have. Didn't think about
it. Sorry."

"Not a problem."

"Speaking of problems, I hope you don't mind;
but I mentioned to Allison that you were here."

He made a slight face, but it was gone quickly. "I probably should have told her myself. Thanks for stopping her from worrying."

"Sure. She had an interesting solution to my problem with my parents." The waiter came by and we gave our orders. Once he left, I continued, "She suggested I have my parents talk to Taria. Do you think that would work?"

Now he was definitely frowning. "Hm. It might. She'd do just about anything to keep the school running smoothly, and right now that means keeping you there. If that means lying to your parents and convincing them I'm a cross between St. Francis of Assisi and Mother Teresa, she will." I giggled at the thought. "You think I'm kidding. I'm not. She could tell them all kinds of things. That I'm the illegitimate son of royalty removed from the realm for my own safety, and so I'm not in competition for the throne. That she thinks I'm in the witness protection program, or that I'm actually a wonderful person, but so severely socially awkward that people get the wrong impression. Or that I'm mildly brain damaged. Basically, pick your story. She'll back you up."

I shook my head. "I don't want to lie to them anymore than I have to. I mentioned you getting hurt last semester, which was a bit of a mistake; then lied and said it was a snowmobile accident, which was an even bigger mistake. They knew I was lying right away."

"So what did you tell them?" Adrian asked, leaning back so the waiter could put down our plates.

I thanked the waiter, then waited until he left. He

seemed a little curious for my tastes. "I said you got jumped, admitted it happened on campus, but they caught the culprit. No details."

"I'll be discrete."

"Thanks." I bit my lip. Yeah, I should probably tell him. "Hey, maybe it's nothing, maybe it's something…"

"Go ahead." He focused all his attention on me.

"I wanted to talk to Jesse this morning, so I went jogging with him. Well, I'm pretty sure I saw the same car drive by three times. A black car with a cracked side mirror, passenger side. Now, maybe it was someone who got lost, or something, but…" I trailed off.

"No, you're right. Pay attention to something like that. I didn't get a sense that you were in danger, but I think it might be best that you avoid going out by yourself more often than necessary."

I huffed in irritation. Bad enough I need guards at Hyde, now home too? "Right. Um, I hate to ask, I really do. But–"

"It wasn't me. I swear."

"Okay. I believe you."

We changed the subject then. I mentioned that Allison might pop down for a visit if she could arrange the time. Adrian's verbal response was non-committal, but he seemed pleased.

I also suggested introducing him to my biology teacher, Linda Green. She was a magicus who graduated from Hyde, and was one of the deciding factors in my choosing that school. Mom may never forgive her for that. Of course, I hadn't known she was a magicus until I came back for Christmas break. Adrian said he'd meet her if I wanted and she didn't mind, but he didn't care much one way or another. It was almost like he didn't expect me to want to introduce him to anyone. Maybe he didn't.

Adrian apologized for causing family strife for me. Since I didn't think that things would be particularly peaceful even if he wasn't here, I accepted his apology and told him it wasn't his fault. I promised to call Taria today and let him know what she said so that we were all consistent. The whole thing made me both realize why and be glad that I usually tried to be honest. Keeping stories straight was exhausting.

"Do your parents know that you're meeting me for lunch?" Adrian asked.

"Yes. I told them when I asked if there were any plans for today. I figured lying about it would just prove to them that you are a 'bad influence' and that I should stay away from you. They made me take Rose's, well, my old, cell phone. I also told them where I was, and I'm supposed to call if we go anywhere else." Seriously I hadn't had restrictions like this since middle school. Probably because in high school, my parents had to push me to socialize. When I did, they were so happy, they seldom cared where I went or how late I stayed. Of course, that wasn't usually me alone with a guy, and never a guy they suspected of having bad, possibly criminal intentions. I should probably be grateful that they were letting me leave the house without a chaperone, a panic button, and a container of pepper spray.

"You're going to go along with this?" Adrian sounded more curious than judging.

"Of course. Far as possible, anyway. The fastest way to get my parents to stop digging into everything and trust me again is to be as trustworthy as possible. I'm not going to go against them unless it's important."

"I wish someone had suggested that to me years ago." Adrian gave a wry smile as he wrapped his hands around his cup.

"Would you have listened then?"

He gave a huff of a laugh. "No, probably not. Let me guess, you were the good kid who never got in trouble."

"I set the kitchen on fire when I was twelve, remember? Trust me; I got in plenty of trouble for that. But I seldom got into major trouble. And never for deliberate disobedience. More like carelessness or forgetfulness."

He laughed at the reminder. "Thanks, I had almost forgotten about that. Any pictures?"

"No. For some *strange* reason, no one thought that my destroying part of the house was worth memorializing." I thought about it some more. "Actually, there might have been a couple pictures taken for insurance purposes, but I doubt we still have them. No, I will not look for them. No, if I do find them, I will not show you. No, you are not going to go telling everyone about my mis-adventures with a chemistry set."

"You are no fun, did you know that?" Adrian shook his head with a smile. A real smile. That made it worth it.

"Yay, my life's purpose is complete." I deliberately kept my voice as dry as possible.

In keeping with my 'curfew', Adrian suggested it would probably be best to get me home early, and insisted on walking me home.

We hadn't gone a block when I spotted a black car with a cracked passenger side mirror. "Adrian…"

"I see it." There was something odd in his voice. Some anger, some resignation. "Stay slightly behind me."

"Okay." The car came to a stop. "Um, any ideas?" I asked, mentally cataloging the nearest public buildings. The storefront next to us was closed, but there was a gas station about fifty yards behind us, and a library across the street. The café was only a little further back.

"I think I know what this is about." He turned his back on the car, put his left hand over his right, and ran his hand down his fingers. A sign we had invented. *Follow my lead.* Then he took his right hand, crossed his first two fingers, and tapped his collar bone briefly. *Intimidation, not yet threat. Act calm.* If he had used three fingers, tapping twice, it would have meant, *Intimidation, not yet threat. Act scared.*

I scratched twice at my ear. *Message received.*

He turned back, muttering under his breath, "Be prepared to run if need be."

"You think it will?"

"No. But be prepared."

He didn't get a chance to say anything more than that. The rear passenger side door opened, and a very large black man, with a small scar running down his neck, climbed out. He was wearing a suit that was clearly tailored for him. Money. But he was also trying, successfully, to be intimidating. Bodyguard? What was going on?

"Mr. Char, you've given us quite the run-around. We need to talk. Miss Peters, you better come too. Get in the car. Both of you."

I looked to Adrian. He nodded and walked forward. "I see Dad still has you running around doing his errands, Ed." He got to the car door and indicated for me to climb in. It was quickly apparent that I would have to slide all the way in, putting me next to the opposite car door. Able to open it, if necessary. Maybe. Who knew what security measures they had on the locks?

Adrian climbed in next to me, while I examined the car. It looked normal from the outside, but was clearly bigger inside, and there was a seat facing ours. The mysterious Ed sat there.

Ed stared at us. I assume so, anyway, because I couldn't tell where he was looking through his sunglasses. He might have been catching a quick nap. The silence was probably meant to intimidate. It was working.

Adrian broke it. "You know, if you are just going to stare, I can give you a picture. You can take it home and whenever you feel mad at me, you can take it out and give it a good glare. When you wear that one out, I'll give you another."

There might almost have been a smile there. "Mr. Char–"

"Violet's not going to be intimidated by your Man in Black routine, and *I* know you're a giant teddy bear. What do you want and why did you follow me a couple thousand miles?"

"I imagine Miss Peters could ask you the same question."

"I missed the dulcet sounds of her voice. If you tell me the same thing, I'm out of the car now." Adrian's voice was so deadpan that it was all I could do not to burst into a fit of hysterical giggles.

Ed did not look so amused. "No, strangely enough, that wasn't what brought me here. We had a deal, Mr. Char. It was agreed that you wouldn't need a security detail at Hyde, and you would have been covered under your father's detail if you stayed home. Since you are nether at Hyde nor at home, you have a security detail. Me."

Security detail? What? I suddenly remembered that Adrian's father and grandfather were famous politically in this dimension's council of whatever they call people who know about the dimensions. So, maybe Adrian rated a bodyguard.

"Now, see, I remember waiving my security detail. Being that I'm over eighteen, I have the right to do that."

"Your father reinstated it." Ed shifted his leg a little, allowing me to see a gun in his sock. It was the first voluntary movement he had made since he climbed in the car.

Adrian huffed in irritation. "Why?"

"All I know is what he told me. To quote, 'Keep my idiot son from getting himself killed or arrested. Keep him out of trouble. As much as possible.' I think your father needs to stop asking me to do the impossible. Or at least pay me better for it."

The car started moving. I'd be lying if I said that didn't alarm me. But Adrian was still calm. "I can take care of myself."

"As I recall, in the past two years, you've ended up requiring major medical attention twice, and minor medical attention on several other occasions. Then you got involved in a group that attracts danger even more than you do. Personally, I think you need a full team following you around at school. However, I am not being paid for that. Nor can you pay me enough for that. Now, out of school, you followed a friend a couple thousand miles, and spooked her parents. May I say how much I appreciate you making my job harder?"

The panther shifter shrugged. "It's a gift. I don't need a security detail. Tell Dad I'm old enough to make that decision."

"Yet he pays me. And he says to keep you, and your lady friend out of trouble."

Adrian's posture didn't shift, his expression was still one of annoyed boredom, but I could feel the tension in him, sparking like lightning. "Dad mentioned Violet?"

"By name and address."

Yup, definitely spooked now. "What is Mr. Char's interest in me? Adrian's father, I mean." Considering Ed kept calling Adrian, 'Mr. Char'. Probably to annoy him.

"Nothing. But your friend, Mr. Char, is interested in you. Hence the older Mr. Char's interest. Meanwhile, I have a few questions for you. In private." The car stopped and the door opened. "Mr. Char, if you will wait outside." It wasn't a request.

Adrian looked at me, and looked at Ed. He twisted an imaginary ring. *It's up to you.*

Gee, thanks, Adrian. Leave it up to me to decide if I want to be alone with the creepy armed bodyguard. Of course, the very fact that he *was* leaving it up to me suggested that he didn't think it was dangerous.

"She can talk to me, or she can talk to Evans." Ed faced me. "A hint for you. You do *not* want to talk to Evans."

Adrian bristled. "Evans is here?"

"Does that surprise you, Mr. Char?" Ed asked, one eyebrow raised just over the brim of his probably very expensive sunglasses.

"If Evans so much as looks at her funny–"

"Then I suggest you let her talk to Ed," A man outside the car said. He was as tall as Ed, but much skinnier, with a shock of wheat blond hair. Outfit was just as expensive. While he didn't seem as intimidating as Ed, somehow, he felt more dangerous.

Adrian gave me one last look. I gave him a nod, and a smile that I didn't feel. Doubt it fooled him, but he climbed out of the car. Then the door shut.

Ed took off his sunglasses. There was a burn mark near his right eye. I really didn't want to know how he got that. "What is your interest in Adrian Char?"

This was going to be fun. I could tell. "He's my friend."

"You've dated a little."

"A little."

"Are you currently dating?"

Honestly, I had no idea. "You'll have to ask

Adrian that."

"What is Adrian Char's interest in you?"

He has a psychic bond to me. And I am *so* not going to say that. This was one of the rare times that I was glad that I was telepath-proof. "You'll have to ask Adrian that."

"Were you aware that the Chars are a very important and influential family?"

"I learned that Adrian's father and grandfather both served in the Hall. There was a note about that in my government textbook." Before that, I hadn't even known that our dimensional government was called 'the Hall'.

"A class you had in your second semester."

I blinked. "Have you been spying on me?"

"Yes."

That was blunt. "Okay. Why?"

"It's my job. Were you aware before that class?"

"No. We don't discuss family much."

"Did your discovering this change anything?"

"No. Should it?"

"It would for some people," Ed said, leaning forward. "It should for you."

"Why?" I shrugged. "My roommate was from a family that is probably equally influential, and she's training to be an ambassador. It was never a factor in our friendship."

"It should matter to you, because if you remain involved with Adrian Char, you will have to live with security and scrutiny at all times. If you cannot accept that, then you should back out now."

I burst out laughing. Ed never cracked a smile, simply waiting until my hysterics had ended. "Sorry. It's just, well, that's basically been my life since I started at school."

Ed nodded. "I am Adrian Char's primary bodyguard. It is my job to keep him safe. If I believe you to be a threat to him, I will remove that threat."

"Are you giving me that shovel speech? Hurt him and I'll bury you?"

A small quirk of a smile. "You could look at it that way. Someone has to."

Right. "If it helps, I have no intention of hurting him. I'm not saying we'll never fight, but he's my friend. Maybe more. We'll see."

Ed measured me with his eyes for another moment. "Very well. You may go, Miss Peters."

Chapter Six

Clearing the Air

The car door opened then. Adrian offered me a hand climbing out of the car, while glaring at the tall man next to him, presumably Evans. He blatantly made sure to stand between us, even when it was awkward. "Come on, let's get you home." Adrian looked around, probably trying to get his bearings. For that matter, I was a little confused too. The area looked industrial, but not very used. Possibly vaguely familiar, but certainly not an area I knew well.

"Miss Peters' house is approximately three blocks that way." Ed pointed to our left. "We'll be around."

I nodded, as Adrian briskly started off away from them. It wouldn't do any good, and we both knew it, but it was the thought that mattered.

The car drove away, but we both knew they were watching. After half a block, Adrian broke the tense silence. "Remind me to buy you a Taser."

I couldn't help it, I laughed until I couldn't breathe anymore. Not that it was that funny, but the nervous energy had to go somewhere. It hurt, but I couldn't stop laughing. Air would be really nice though.

Adrian gave me a funny look. "You're turning red. No, seriously, breathe. Are you alright?"

Not being able to talk, I just nodded.

"Not very believable."

"I'm," gasp, "okay."

"Right. Good. I meant it about getting you a Taser, though. You'd actually use one if you had to, right?"

I had to think about it. "If I absolutely, really had to? I think I could. Probably. But I can't have one at Hyde though, can I?"

"No rule against it."

"Wow, that's odd. Most schools have strict rules about weapons."

Adrian scanned the area. No pedestrians nearby, and even car traffic was light. "Most schools don't have so many students with natural weapons. If you actually used it on campus, there would be a hearing where you would have to justify your usage, but that's typical for anyone using offensive force of any kind."

A black car with a cracked passenger side mirror glided past. We ignored it. "So, security detail?"

"Yeah, I've had one on and off for most of my life. Ed's been my primary for about fifteen years."

"Um, he didn't seem to like you much."

Adrian smirked. "Don't fall for his act. He's a big softy. Sure, he wants to strangle me sometimes, but most people who know me do. He may care more about my safety than Dad does." I choked at that. "Okay, that might not be fair. I'm not saying Dad wants anything to happen to me; but he's more concerned about whether or not I'm causing a scandal or making him look bad than my personal safety and wellbeing."

"Oh." Yeah, really not sure I want to know more about the Char family situation. "When you say he's a teddy bear…"

A true smile. "Yeah, Kodiak."

"What about Evans?"

The smile fled. "Him you want to stay away from. Ed is in the business to protect people. Evans is in the business because it gives him an excuse to be a bully." Despite the fact that the nearest pedestrian was still more than a block away, Adrian lowered his voice. "He's almost *magical* that way."

"Got it. Are they always partners?"

"Usually, but not always. Complimentary abilities."

I nodded. "Oh, hey, I know where we are now." Still wasn't an area I was very familiar with, but I was at least confident we were going the right direction.

"Good. So, what did Ed say?"

"He wanted to make sure I wasn't playing fast and loose with your heart."

Adrian missed the next curb and almost fell on his face. "What?"

"You okay?"

"What did you say?" He kept walking without looking where he was going. I had to tug him sideways so he didn't walk into a telephone pole.

"Would you pay attention? You're going to get hurt."

Adrian came to a complete stop, doing a passable imitation of the immovable object. I didn't feel like playing the unstoppable force today. Nor did I really want to know what happened when an unstoppable force met an immovable object. Probably nothing good. "He asked if I was aware of your family background, how long I had been aware, if it changed anything, etc. Oh, and he said that being your bodyguard, he was hired to remove threats to your safety, so I'd better not make him think I was one."

"Did he threaten you?" Was Adrian growling? He sure sounded like he was growling.

I shrugged. "Only if I hurt you. It's the shovel speech. I'm sure you're familiar with it." Adrian looked at me blankly. "It's when the people who care about someone tell the person dating that someone that if he, or she, hurts that person… Wait. Stop. That's confusing. Okay, person A is dating person B. Person C is a relative or good friend of person B and tells person A that they'll bury him, or her, if A hurts B. Usually in a metaphorical sense. Okay?"

Adrian shook his head. "He said that? Really?"

"Well, a fair bit of it was implied. Haven't you ever done something like that for Allison's dates?"

Part of me was curious what that evil smirk meant. The rest of me really, really didn't want to know. "Maybe. Something like that. Still, sorry he threatened you."

"It's fine. It just tells me someone's looking out for you. I know you probably put up with a few versions of the speech." Ilse for certain. Probably Tim, as well. Maybe Kara. Wouldn't put it have past Jesse, either. "Allison never gave me the speech."

"Yeah, well, Allison adores you."

I blinked. "Really?"

"Sure, didn't you know that?" Adrian gave me a weird look.

"Well, she's very friendly, but she's like that with everyone. She's almost as outgoing as Kara."

"No, she really isn't. I mean, she isn't anti-social," the 'like I am' came through clearly if silently, "But she's friendly with the group because of me, and you. She's glad to have made friends with everyone, but she wouldn't have if it wasn't for us."

I wanted to ask 'why me', but the answer slapped me in the face before I could open my mouth and make a fool of myself. She cared because Adrian had a bond with me. "How much is her liking me is because of you?"

"It's not. That's how she met you, and I'm sure she would have tried to like you because of me. But do you remember the first time you met her?"

"I remember the kestrel dive bombing you." That wasn't something one forgot quickly. Then the kestrel turned into Allison. Who shook my hand and made an unsettling prediction. That was fun. Not.

"Then she shanghaied me to help her move her stuff."

That took me a moment longer. "Yeah, I think I remember that."

"One of the first things she said was how much she liked you. I think I was ten the last time she approved of one of my friends before that."

"But... She... I only talked to her for a couple minutes. And shook her hand."

"That was part of it. Part of it was things I told her. A large part was that you didn't freak out and get me in trouble. She thinks you're good for me." Adrian wasn't looking at me, and his ears seemed a little pink.

If he could say it, I could. "I think you may be good for me, too. I just have to convince my family that."

We didn't say anything the rest of the way home.

***

I sat on the top of the stairs, just out of sight of the living room. For information gathering. Okay, I was eavesdropping. Not something I was proud of, but it wasn't like I could make myself stop. Mom and Dad were in the living room, talking to Taria on speakerphone. I had to make sure our stories matched up. Plus, I was honestly curious what she would say.

"Thank you for agreeing to talk to us, Ms. Clay," Mom started. When I had asked what I should say her name was, she said she generally went by Taria Clay in this dimension. According to her, it was because she was as old as dirt. I don't think she's that old, but it was funny. I had been worried about the language spell, but Taria said it wasn't a problem. One, all phones in Hyde are enchanted to allow the person on each end to hear what the language they expected to hear. Two, Taria had been around for a very long time, and apparently had a hobby of learning languages. So she knew English. Not the most modern form, but pretty close. Hopefully if there were any differences, they would chalk it up to her being an academic.

"You can call me Taria. And it's no bother. I consider providing guidance for students and their families to be the most important part of my job."

"Do you advise a lot of students?" Dad asked. "Do you actually remember Violet?"

"Violet and Adrian both. The two of them have made quite an impression."

"That's a little of what we're afraid of," Mom said.

Taria laughed. "Don't worry. They both did very well this year. I admit that Adrian ran into some difficulty that year before, so I can understand your concern. But since meeting your daughter; he's turned completely around. He does better in school, gets along better with students, and is more helpful to the faculty. I didn't know Violet before, so it's a little harder to figure out his influence on her; but as the school year moved on, she did better in her studies, participated in more extra-curricular activities, etc. Both of them are also part of a group of students who have done a lot of volunteer work at the school." That was what we agreed to call the fact that we caught people trying to sabotage the school on two occasions. It sounded less dangerous, and I didn't have to tell my parents how near I came to being killed.

"I see," Mom said. "Neither of them have been particularly forthcoming about things that happened at school."

"Did either of them mention that, due to the nature of some things studied in our science department, and a few other places; many of the happenings in the school are covered under non-disclosure agreements?" I had used that as a cover story last Christmas. Taria loved it, saying she was going to use it in the future.

"Violet did say that. Do you think we should be alarmed by the fact that this boy crossed a few thousand miles, and country borders, on a whim, to see our daughter?" Dad asked.

Rose came out of her room then. I held a finger to my lips. Puzzled, she came to the steps to listen.

"It was an impetuous move, I admit. But please keep in mind their age. It is not uncommon for people that age to do impulsive things. As for alarming? I have seen the two of them together, and I do not believe either would ever deliberately hurt the other."

"Adrian stalked Violet. They both admit that. Why didn't the school do anything?" Dad asked.

"I actually spoke to Violet about that very issue shortly before they came to an understanding. Adrian Char showed no signs of harming, or meaning to harm, Violet. The school could do nothing unless Violet chose to report it. I cannot, will not, impinge on Adrian's privacy, but I can reassure you as I reassured her that his intentions were not harmful. Luckily, they managed to work things out themselves soon after."

Rose took a seat next to me.

"How can you be so certain?" Mom asked.

"I mentioned that Adrian… had a few issues the previous year. As a result, he was required to have regular meetings with me, and with one of the school's counselors over this last year. I cannot say much more about those sessions, and I strongly recommend against asking Adrian about them, but I feel I have a good understanding of Adrian Char."

"So, you think we should just let them be?" Mom asked.

"Probably for the best. Any other questions?"

There was a pause. "No, I think we're good for now. Can we call you if we have more questions?" Dad asked.

"Certainly. I look forward to it."

Rose and I quickly and quietly retreated, in case Mom or Dad came upstairs. They didn't.

Before I shut my door, I heard Mom say, "So, we just trust them?"

"For now," Dad agreed. "Violet will tell us if there's something important."

I would have appreciated it so much more if I didn't feel like I was betraying their trust.

***

Adrian called me early the next morning. "Hey, Violet. I got some visitor passes to Colonial Williamsburg. I remember you saying you liked visiting there. Would you like to go? Maybe some of your family?"

How did he get passes?" "I'll have to ask. *I'm* definitely interested. Thank you. How many passes do you have?"

Even over the phone, I could almost see him shrug. "Five. I think Ed is trying to make it up to you for threatening you. Or up to me for threatening you."

"They'll follow us."

"They'd do that anyway. You still in?"

I huffed a laugh. "Yeah, you're right. I'm still in. Let me see who's interested."

"Okay, call me back in about twenty minutes? I'm going to breakfast."

I went down to find Dad getting ready to leave. Okay, so he wouldn't be going. Oh, school day. Rose would be gone. No, she was in the kitchen. "Why aren't you in school?"

"Teacher in-service day. Can we do something cool?"

"Maybe. Where's Mom?"

"She had to leave already." Dad took another sip of coffee while packing up his briefcase.

"Oh, drat. Um, Adrian called. He got passes to Colonial Williamsburg for me and any of my family who wanted to come."

Rose perked up. She loved Colonial Williamsburg. "Ooh, ooh! Can I go?"

Dad frowned. "I don't know. I don't like the idea of you two going out of town alone with him. Wait, Charlie's got a teacher in-service day too, doesn't she?"

"Dad, we go to the same school," Rose said.

"And Jesse finished exams last week. Okay, if Charlie and Jesse, or at least Jesse, go too, then you can go." He turned to me. "Will that be alright with Adrian? They are his passes."

"Probably. I'm supposed to call him back in," I checked my watch, "about fifteen minutes. Let me check with him before we call Uncle Jack and Aunt Laura."

Adrian agreed, even if he wasn't thrilled by Jesse's inclusion. At least he didn't seem reluctant to meet Charlie, Jesse's younger sister. "She's Rose's age. They'll probably stick together. And yes, they'll tease and giggle. Fortunately, we can distract them by pointing out horses and stuff." Jesse would be a little harder.

Once that was settled, I called Jesse. He wasn't big on history, and even less interested in spending the day with Adrian and me; but he agreed, supposedly to protect Rose and Charlie. I must have forfeited most of my protection by insisting on hanging out with Adrian. Jesse also offered to borrow his mom's van, allowing us to transport five people in one vehicle. Considering what parking was like at Colonial Williamsburg, I was quick to agree. Hopefully Adrian wouldn't mind that. I wasn't sure if Adrian had a car here. Or even at home.

I called Adrian back, and he agreed to Jesse's offer as well. "No, my car won't fit five comfortably, I don't think. It's a rental. I *might* be able to fit four." He paused. "It there anything in particular you wanted to see while there? I really don't know much about the place."

"Don't worry, there will be plenty of suggestions. Bring a camera if you have one. And wear comfortable shoes. There's a lot of walking."

We left at eleven. Jesse drove, with me riding shotgun. Rose and Charlie piled into the way back seat, whispering and giggling; with Adrian sitting in the seat between them and the front. I'm sure he could hear every word they were saying, but he was politely trying to ignore it. Either that, or he really didn't want to get involved in young teenage girl talk. Especially since he was one of the main topics of conversation.

We got lunch on the way, since it would be cheaper than eating there. Not by much, both Williamsburg and Newport News have a 13.5 percent tax on restaurant food.

Finding a parking spot was easier than anticipated, probably because it was a school day. Adrian handed out the passes, and soon we were walking up Duke of Gloucester Street.

"Ooh, can we check out the shops?" Charlie asked, pointing out the Merchant's Square souvenir shops.

"We can do that on the way back," Jesse said.

"Yeah. If you buy something, you don't want to carry it around all day," I pointed out. The girls reluctantly agreed.

"Okay, we're all going to stick together. No running off, no disappearing. If we do that, no one should get lost." Jesse eyed all of us, giving Adrian and me particularly measuring looks. It didn't feel fair to me.

"On the off chance we do end up separated, I

think we should probably meet at the Governor's Palace. It's the most recognizable building here," I suggested.

The girls nodded, Adrian shrugged, and Jesse glowered. "Okay. But we aren't going to *get* separated."

"Where is the Governor's Palace?" Adrian asked.

"I'll point it out. You can't miss it. In fact, that should definitely be on our list to see," I said.

"Yeah! Maybe they'll be giving the harpsicord demonstration," Charlie enthused.

"The harpsicord is neat. Personally, I prefer the glass armonica," I said. I don't know how frequently they do it, but I saw a glass armonica demonstration here a couple years ago and had been fascinated. Benjamin Franklin was credited with inventing the unusual instrument.

"I want to see the animals," Rose said. "Horse, chickens, cows, and sheep. Hey, it's lambing season, isn't it? Maybe there'll be babies."

"Maybe," Jesse answered. "Can't hurt to take a look."

We started down Duke of Gloucester, looking at the historically restored houses, the historically clothed re-enactors, and hundreds of tourists. Most of Colonial Williamsburg is built along Duke of Gloucester, with everything within walking distance. The main problem is crowds. Going early, late, during school hours, or not during tourist season helps, but the town itself is always open to tourists. There's even ghost tours at night.

"Look, a carriage," Rose pointed out. We moved a little more to the side, letting the black glossy horse-drawn carriage, pulled by a pair of dapple gray horses, through. "I want to take a carriage ride someday."

I glared at Rose since she was glancing at Adrian when she said it. "Maybe someday you will. But not today." Those were expensive. True, Adrian didn't pay for these passes, but she didn't know that, and if he had, he would have been spending a *lot* of money already today. It certainly wasn't fair to hint he should spend more.

That, however, somehow got Jesse involved. Male competition? I really didn't know. "Carriage ride, huh? Well, tickets usually sell out early, but let's see what they've got."

I winced and silently prayed they were sold out. They weren't. Jesse's smile looked more like something that belonged on a shark than a friendly expression. "Well, since Violet's *friend* was kind enough to invite us all here, I think I can pay for carriage ride tickets. You don't mind horses, right, Adrian?"

Adrian's smile was as friendly as Jesse's. "Not at all. That's very generous of you."

They might not have sold out of tickets, but the closest reservation wasn't until three. It was currently just after twelve. I tried to take the practical approach. "Well, we should be able to see most of the city before then." I scanned around, looking for something, anything, to change the subject. "Who wants to see the weaver?"

We went to see the weaver, even though I'm not sure anyone cared. The girls were too excited about a carriage ride. Jesse and Adrian were switching back and forth between trying to mentally incinerate each other and ignoring the other's existence. I just wanted a distraction. That said, *I* thought it was interesting enough. I loved watching demonstrations on how they did things back then.

They were upfront about the fact that there was no evidence that weaving was actually done in Williamsburg at the time, with most of the cloth being imported. But if it was done, then this was how they would have done it. There were samples of wool and flax in different colors and stages of development. Jars of different things used to dye the materials were situated around the room, including the beetles needed to get red.

Shortly after the weaver, we came across a major side street. Adrian scanned the very large, very grand building that was prominent at the end of said side street. "Let me guess, that's the Governor's Palace?"

"Yup. You should see it during the Grand Illumination," I said.

"Yeah, you missed it this year," Rose pouted.

"Sorry, it was before I got off for Christmas break." Adrian looked confused. "First Sunday in December. They light the place up and do fireworks. It's a pretty big deal here. That and First Night. New Year's Eve." I tried very hard not to blush, thinking about New

Year's. "This place is really neat around Christmas. All houses, even the privately owned ones, have to use historically accurate decorations, so the wreaths get fascinating. Fruit and other greenery for the most part."

Bruton Parrish was our next stop. There were no services going on, so the public was allowed in. "This is the oldest church in continual use in the country," Rose said. I vaguely remembered her doing a report on Bruton Parrish a couple years, so let her show off her knowledge.

The pews were surrounded by small walls, with a gate that could be locked from the inside. I'm sure there was a good reason for it, probably warmth, but I always imagined it was to keep everyone in their seats until the sermon was over. On the gate doors were written the names of famous parishioners, who presumably used those pews before. Richard Henry Lee, Thomas Jefferson, George Washington, and many others.

We pointed out various names we recognized. About the third time we pointed out a name Adrian didn't know, Jesse turned to him. "Are you really interested in American history at all?"

He shrugged. "Some. Sure I don't know as much of it as you do, but it's always interesting to touch the past. Besides, I'll bet I know more Canadian history than you do. Probably more British history too."

"Is Canada still under British Rule?" Charlie asked.

"Sort of. We're part of the Commonwealth, with the Queen as the head. But in reality, all governing is done by Canadian elected officials."

"Is Canada a lot different from the U.S.?" Rose asked.

"Couldn't say. I haven't seen much of the U.S. This part is definitely different. Geographically if nothing else. But I'm sure states closer to the border are much more similar. Also, both Canada and the United States are very big countries. There's a lot of variety."

We hit the basket weaver and the rare chicken exhibit, the fact that one of the breeds was called a Dorking caused a couple muffled giggles, before we got to the Governor's Palace.

"For rare chicken breeds, they don't look that different from any other chickens I've seen," Adrian muttered.

"You should see the sheep," I told him.

"Oh, what do they look like?"

"Sheep. White ones."

The Governor's Palace was as lavishly furnished on the inside as it was grand on the outside. Obviously the home of someone of importance. The entrance hall was lined with bayonet-tipped muskets. The parlor, the furthest most guests would have been allowed to enter, shared the same decorating scheme to impress, and probably intimidate.

While we couldn't go in the pantry, we were

allowed to peek in. It was huge, probably a necessity considering how many people would have had to work there when the house was occupied. On display were china and glassware, possibly authentic from the era.

"The colors are rich. The walls, I mean. I just… wasn't expecting quite this much," Adrian said as we looked over the rope barrier into a mint green bedroom.

"Yeah, they seemed to really love color here. The Virginians were definitely not Quakers," I agreed.

We moved into the ballroom painted Prussian Blue. It was just a shade or two from the blue that was so common here that it was called Williamsburg Blue.

"He's doing the harpsichord demonstration!" Rose squealed.

Sure enough, a re-enactor of musician Peter Pelham was playing the harpsichord. He explained how the instrument had strings inside that were plucked, like one might do to a guitar. As a result, the notes were always the same volume, in contrast to the *new* instrument, the *Pianoforte*, or 'soft-loud', that had strings that were struck, but the volume could be adjusted by the pedals. "A nice enough instrument, but it will never replace the harpsichord." His 'prediction' caused a few giggles.

Moving out of the Governor's Palace, Charlie suddenly caught our attention. "Look, geese! And a duck. Maybe he's lost."

There was a group of about five or six Canada

geese and one mallard duck, waddling up the street like they owned it. "That's the Duck of Gloucester." I couldn't resist the pun.

I got several groans for that, but Adrian chuckled. Of course, he also had his eyes skyward. I followed his gaze, spotting an American Kestrel on top of a nearby roof. *Hello, Allison, I didn't expect you here so soon.* I met Adrian's eyes, raised an eyebrow and gave a slight head jerk to the bird. Adrian nodded.

Not that Allison was the only one following us. I had spotted Ed a few times, and I think Evans was part of our tour group in the Palace. Judging by the way Adrian glared at him, I was right. Not that either of us mentioned any of them.

"Are the Canadian geese looking for you?" Jesse asked Adrian.

"It's Canada geese, actually. Common mistake." Adrian shrugged at the questioning looks he got. "My sister likes birds." Then he addressed the birds. "I'll be back in Canada before you are!"

"Especially if they're here during the summer. These guys are probably permanent residents. Speaking of Canada, they also have Canadian horses here." I looked at the map. "But we won't get there if we don't get moving."

Next stop was the magazine, where they kept the weapons and gunpowder. There were a few more demonstrations of various trades, and then the post office. The post office was in actual operation. Not only could you buy postcards and other touristy stuff, but letters and postcards were hand cancelled and sent out. Adrian made us wait a few minutes so he could send Allison a postcard. I wasn't sure why he was bothering, since she was following us, but hey, he was having fun. Maybe I'd come back at some point and send some postcards to others in the group.

There was a very brief stop to say hi to the Canadian horses, who loved Adrian. We claimed it was because he smelled Canadian. Though he was more likely to smell like a large cat. I couldn't pick up the scent, but we knew polar bears could. No idea how well horses could smell. Whatever the case, they kept trying to eat his hair and coat. Yes, even in our eighty plus degree weather, Adrian was wearing his customary black duster. Well, if it was charmed to keep him warm, maybe it was charmed to keep him cool. Did earn him the occasional look, though.

"What is with these horses?" Adrian asked, moving further from the fence.

"Could be worse. Remember visiting Tim's family?" Tim's family had pet polar bears. For reasons we do not know, polar bears, at least in that dimension, really don't like cats. Adrian didn't appreciate being chased around by them any better.

Adrian winced at the reminder. "Right, let's go. We're running low on time."

He was right, but we still took a long look at the sheep. There were indeed a few lambs. The girls cooed and cheered, and most of us took a couple pictures.

It was close, but we made it back to the carriage ride meeting place in time. Then there was a little trouble with the seating arrangements. The carriage wasn't quite big enough for five, but we could squish. The problem was Jesse. He didn't want me sitting next to Adrian, didn't want to sit next to Adrian himself, and was adamant against letting either of the girls sit next to him. Since they weren't going to let Adrian sit next to the driver, Jesse was out of luck. I sat next to Adrian, while Jesse squashed between the girls.

"Can we pet the horses?" Charlie asked.

"Not while they're working. Sorry," The driver said with the air of one who answered that question a lot.

The ride began. The girls started whispering about something and giggling. Jesse was doing a series of very interesting facial contortions as he tried to contain himself. Between that and the glances they kept casting in our direction, I would have known what they were talking about even if I wasn't catching the occasional word or phrase. Adrian, who could probably hear every word, was resolutely watching the passing scenery.

"How did you meet Violet?" Charlie asked.

Adrian turned to her in surprise. "We go to the same school."

"I know. But how did you meet her?"

"I ran into her in the cafeteria."

"Actually, I nearly ran into you. Literally. Twice.

It was my first night. I was a little out of it," I corrected.

"Was it? I didn't know that," Adrian said. "How long had you been there?"

"Less than two hours, I think."

Adrian laughed. "That explains a couple things. You must have been... overwhelmed."

Jesse tried, unsuccessfully, to suppress a shiver. Probably remembering his own first day and what a shock finding out the truth had been. Of course, I was luckier than him. I was there at least a day before being attacked or witnessing an attack.

"I *was* overwhelmed. And jetlagged. And then you just *stared* at me." I snickered. "I tried, awkwardly, I admit, to introduce myself, and you didn't say anything."

"I told you my name." Adrian smirked.

"*After* I started walking away."

"Why didn't you talk to her? I mean, I know she's weird and all–"

"Thanks, Rose."

"You're welcome. But still, you shouldn't have been able to tell how weird she was at first glance."

Adrian let out a breath slowly. "I... Well, it was weird. You've heard of love at first sight?"

The girls nodded and leaned forward. Jesse

glowered.

"It wasn't quite like that. I didn't know anything about her. But I saw her, and I just *knew* there was something special about her. So, yes, I may have accidentally been a little rude to her, but it wasn't because I didn't like her. I was trying to figure out what was going on. Why I felt that way." Nice cover story. He couldn't tell him that he recognized that I was the person he was bonded to as a defender psychic.

Rose leaned back with a happy sigh and a goofy grin. Charlie leaned forward excitedly. Jesse glowered some more. "Then what happened?" Charlie asked.

"It's a small school. We were going to run into each other again," I said.

"Especially if one person seeks out the other. Which I did later. But as it happens, I saw her the next day."

"He kept me from falling on my face down a set of concrete stairs. That would have been very painful." I turned to Adrian. "I did thank you, didn't I?"

"You did."

"Good."

"Did you make a better impression the second time?" Rose asked.

"Him or me? Either way, the answer is probably no." I had been badly startled, and could barely pull myself together to thank him. He had shown incredible reflexes and grace, but acted gruff and disappeared with barely a word.

"I was still confused. Wasn't sure what I was feeling, wasn't sure I wanted to feel it. Violet had just barely escaped a serious injury and was fighting shock."

"It took a few weeks for us to get into the proper groove," I said.

"So, are you dating?" Charlie asked.

Good question. *Very* good question.

Adrian seemed to stumble for words for a minute. He looked at Charlie, intimidated in a way I hadn't seen since he had a polar bear growling at him. Then he looked at me, as if hoping I'd rescue him from the question. I raised my eyebrow and said nothing. I wanted to know too. There were times I'd think yes, then times we seemed to be no more than friends.

"Yes, are you dating Violet?" Jesse asked.

"That…" Adrian swallowed. "That is a very good question." He turned to me. "Violet Peters, will you do me the honor of being my girlfriend?"

Chapter Seven

The Sharp Side of Love

I ignored the squeals; ignored the fact that Jesse looked very much like he wanted to push Adrian out of the carriage, preferably in front of the horses; ignored how even our driver had turned partially to see what was going to happen next. All I looked at was Adrian. I could feel his fear, his hope, and a few other feelings I couldn't decipher.

"Are you sure? Ignoring the peanut gallery over there, are you sure this is something you want?" I asked.

"Violet–" Jesse tried to speak.

"I'm certain. Absolutely certain."

"I–" couldn't stop smiling this absolutely *stupid* smile. "Yes, I would love to be your girlfriend."

"Here's your stop, folks. Congratulations to the both of you."

Jesse jumped off and was storming away before the carriage even came to a complete stop. "Let's go home."

The driver watched him storm away, and shook his head. Probably glad Jesse didn't hurt himself and threaten to sue. It would have been Jesse's own fault, but I doubt Colonial Williamsburg wanted to deal with it. He gave me a wry smile. "Good luck to the both of you, too."

"Thanks. We'll need it!" I called over my shoulder, while chasing after Jesse. Vaguely, I could hear Adrian talking to the driver about tips behind me. Good, at least one of us was on top of things.

Charlie and Rose balked at Jesse's demand to leave immediately. They wanted to see the stores, maybe a few other displays, perhaps photograph each other in the stocks. Jesse wasn't having it. "We're going home. Now."

"But we aren't finished seeing the town, and you said we could see the shops," Charlie whined.

"I changed–" Jesse cut off as I grabbed his arm and started to drag him away.

"Excuse us a moment." I took Jesse a few feet away. We could still see everyone, but there was a small modicum of privacy. Very small, so I spoke quietly. "Yes, I am well aware of your opinion of my decision. I have no doubt that someone; be it you, Rose, or even Charlie, will tell my parents everything before I have a chance to. But sulking like a toddler who needs a nap won't change a thing."

"Sulki–"

I interrupted again. "We have passes to Colonial Williamsburg. They are one day passes. We are *here*, at Colonial Williamsburg. We might as well take advantage of those facts. Not spoil the girls' day because you are in a snit. Besides, look at it this way; as long as we're here, you *know* where we are and exactly what we're doing."

Jesse growled at me.

"C'mon. I'll let you take a picture of me in the stocks."

"What about Adrian?"

"I'm not making any promises on his behalf."

"Fine. But you two…"

"We'll behave ourselves."

We rejoined the rest of the group then. "Okay, we'll stay a little longer. Next stop, the stocks!" Jesse announced.

Everyone took a turn in the stocks for make-believe crimes. Thanks to Jesse, mine was poor decision making and Adrian's was corruption of the innocent. I claimed Jesse's crime was being an overbearing, meddling busybody. Rose was accused of gossip, and Charlie of sloth.

There were a few more stops. My favorites were the silversmith and the apothecary. There were real, expensive, silver pieces for sale at the silversmith, but the apothecary was more things to look at. Then again, we probably didn't want to buy medicines of the day.

Last stop was the Merchant's Village shops. I picked up some postcards while listening to Rose and Charlie try to persuade a reluctant Adrian to buy a tricorner hat. "You know, we should have gotten some root beer or ginger ale." They made old fashioned styles of each, in glass bottles with a little history of brewing in the colonies on the label. I had a collection of bottles by now.

"Yeah, see if you can find some," Jesse suggested, reaching for his wallet. "Who wants what?"

"I got this one," I said, getting the orders. Three root beers, two ginger ales. It wasn't hard to find a seller, but I wasn't allowed to take the drinks back inside the shop. Everyone joined me outside, with Adrian wearing a tri-cornered hat. "So they did talk you into it?"

Adrian shrugged. "Guess they did. I got the woman's cap for Allison. She'll like it. Actually, she probably won't. But she'll wear it because I got it for her." He grabbed a couple bottles before I lost my grip.

I laughed. "Yeah, I've got one too." I passed out the rest. "If anyone doesn't want their bottle, I collect them."

Adrian examined his bottle, reading the label. "No offence, but I may keep this one."

"No problem. I have lots. In fact, you can have mine, too. If you want." He had ginger ale and I had root beer. The history tidbits were different. When I first started, the bottles were different colors, but now they were both brown.

"Can we go now?" Jesse asked.

I rolled my eyes. Then smiled at the squirrel

carefully approaching us, obviously hoping for food. "Hey, critter. Don't have any food for you. Sorry."

Everyone looked where I was looking. Adrian carefully checked his pockets. "I might have, ah, here." He pulled out a small package of peanut butter crackers. "Probably not the healthiest for you, but I'm sure you've had worse." He broke off a piece and tossed it. Now encouraged, the squirrel came closer. By the end of the cracker, he was eating out of Adrian's hand. Honestly, I was a little jealous.

"Careful, squirrel. They're making Brunswick stew at Chowning Tavern," I joked.

Adrian gave me a puzzled look. "What's Brunswick stew?"

"Colonial dish. Traditionally made with squirrel."

"They still do that," Rose said. "Dad said so."

I laughed. "He was teasing you. They don't use squirrel. I think they use chicken. A lot easier to get than squirrel, and you can guarantee quality."

Rose looked at me doubtfully. "Are you sure?"

"Pretty sure. Think about it, do you know how hard it would be to keep squirrel stocked? It's just a joke." There *was* the possibility that the stew used rabbit, but I didn't see the need to tell Rose or Charlie that.

"Oh, look at the bird." Charlie pointed, before looking at the squirrel. "Maybe you should run. That looks like a hawk."

"Kestrel, actually," Adrian said, shading his eyes to look.

Three guesses who *that* was. I cast a side glance at Jesse, but he didn't seem to make the connection. Come to think of it, he might not know Allison's form. Still, if it was Allison, the squirrel was probably safe for the moment. I had no idea if Allison would hunt while in kestrel form, but even if she did, it probably wouldn't be in front of us.

We left soon after. Jesse didn't say a word during the half-hour drive, while the girls wouldn't stop giggling. I kept catching words like 'carriage' and 'romantic'. Judging from the way Jesse's fingers were white on the steering wheel, I was pretty sure he heard them too.

We dropped Adrian off first. I walked him to his room, promising I'd stay outside where I could be seen.

"Is this going to cause trouble for you with your family?" Adrian asked.

I shrugged. "Maybe. Probably. But it might be better this way. At least they know we aren't trying to hide anything."

"I didn't mean to cause trouble."

"The trouble was there. We couldn't have avoided it. It was only a matter of degree. You did mean it, didn't you? Not just for an audience?" I was pretty certain of his answer, but I needed to hear it.

"I meant it if you did."

"I did."

Adrian gave me a crooked grin. "I probably could have thought of a better way to ask you to be my girlfriend."

"Oh, I don't know. The carriage ride scored several points. Of course, the peanut gallery's involvement…"

He laughed. "So, since I asked you to be my girlfriend, may I kiss you?"

"That depends. Is this to annoy Jesse, or because you want to?"

"Both?"

I giggled.

"Mostly the second. Irritating your cousin is a side benefit."

"I can go with that."

Adrian smiled softly, caressed my face and leaned in for a soft, tender kiss. I wasn't sure how I was still standing when he leaned back. "I'll see you later."

"Right. Um, bye, Adrian." I think I floated back to the car. On my face was a dumb goofy grin that probably made me look like an imbecile, and I couldn't even bring myself to care. Not when Jesse took off in a move that probably scraped rubber off the tires; not when the girls couldn't stop giggling and exclaiming about what they saw; not even when we got home and everyone burst in to tell Mom and Dad what happened.

I will admit though, that the thunderous looks on their faces did break through some of that giddy ecstasy.

***

Dad picked up the phone when it rang, listened for maybe ten seconds, said, "Wrong number," and hung up. It was the third time the phone had rung in thirty minutes, and I was getting a little suspicious.

"Who was it?" I asked when Dad came in the living room.

"Wrong number." Dad didn't even look at me.

I had been relieved that there hadn't been a big fight yesterday when they found out that Adrian had asked me to be his girlfriend and I had accepted. Perhaps my relief was a little premature. Things were very tense at home. In fact, I think Dad was postponing a trip he was supposed to be on.

Of course, it *could* be a wrong number. A very persistent wrong number. Dad went back to his newspaper. I got up.

"Where are you going?" Dad asked.

"Kitchen. I need some water."

He grunted, and went back to the paper. Once in the kitchen, I grabbed a glass, started running the tap, and checked the caller ID on the phone. The last three numbers were identical. And slightly familiar. I checked the number Adrian had given me for his hotel room. Sure enough, they were a match.

"Violet, what are you doing?" Dad had come up behind me without my noticing. He shut off the water. "Why are you snooping?"

Trying to take the offensive, huh? Not a bad strategy. Too bad I was angry, not ashamed. "Because apparently I need to. Wrong number?"

"I'm trying to protect you."

"Yeah, see, here's what I don't get. You said you'd give Adrian a chance. You said you'd try. You gave me rules about what I could and couldn't do around him. I agreed. *And I followed those rules!* I told you every time I was meeting with him. Jesse, Charlie, and Rose all came to Williamsburg with us. I have been as honest as possible, and now you're lying to me! You didn't even say, 'No, you can't date him, you can't see him'. You're just lying to keep us apart. Honesty goes both ways."

"You never said you were dating," Dad said.

"We went on a couple dates in school. As for not telling you he asked me to become his girlfriend, I didn't have the chance. There was a Greek Chorus that beat me to it."

Dad gave a small smile before going serious again. "If we said you couldn't see him, would you stop?"

I took a deep breath. I really, really didn't want to make that choice. "We go to the same school; we're part of the same group of friends. We couldn't avoid each other if we wanted to. But I *can* agree not to meet with him here." It would hurt. But I think Adrian would understand. "But didn't you say you'd *try*?"

"That was before he became your boyfriend," Dad grumbled.

"Isn't that an even better reason to try to like him? Or at least get to know him?"

"You said you'd keep in mind that he might not have your best interests in mind."

"I have. But so far, I've seen nothing to back that up."

The phone rang again. I was still holding it, so it was easy to read the number. "It's Adrian." Dad sighed, but didn't say or do anything to stop me from answering it. "Hi, Adrian."

"Hey, Violet. Had some trouble getting in touch with you."

"Yeah, I gathered that. How are you?"

"Fine. Allison is in town for a couple days, would like to see you."

"I'd like to see her too."

"Great. Meet tomorrow for lunch?"

"Hang on, I'll check." I turned to Dad. "Adrian's sister, Allison, is in town. She wants to see me. Any plans for lunch tomorrow?"

"Invite them both to dinner tomorrow," Mom said, surprising us as she came into the kitchen. I hadn't even known she was downstairs. "I want to meet this Allison."

"Okay." I turned back to the phone. "Mom says you're both invited to dinner tomorrow."

I could hear voices on the other side of the line. "Sure. What time and what should we bring?"

Checking with Mom, I spoke again, "Seven o'clock, and you don't have to bring anything."

More sounds on the other side. "Allison says to ask if we can bring a dessert."

I repeated the question. Mom frowned, but nodded. "That's fine."

"Great. See you then. Probably best not to push things."

"I agree. Goodnight, Adrian."

"Night."

***

Dinner with both Char siblings was less awkward and uncomfortable than dinner with just Adrian was. Partially because Jesse wasn't there making subtle digs and generally being difficult. Partially because Allison rose to the occasion, apparently wanting to meet my family.

I hadn't realized it before, but Allison had a gift for controlling the conversation without seeming too. Ilse could do that too, I had seen her do it more than once. Usually, it was only when I was thinking about it afterwards that I realized what she had done. Allison wasn't quite as subtle about it, or I had gotten better at recognizing it. Either way, I could tell what she was doing during dinner itself. But it was working, so I kept my mouth shut.

Perhaps it wasn't a surprise that both of them had this gift. They were both the only daughters of influential political families. So, the most surprising thing would probably be that Adrian *couldn't* maneuver a conversation. Or maybe he could, but seldom bothered.

Whatever the case may be, Allison was a flurry of friendly enthusiasm, bringing up things I didn't remember telling her. She listened, seemingly fascinated, to Rose's stories of school; to Mom's tales about the house she was showing, and to Dad's adventures about traveling to persuade people to buy paper from his company. I could almost see defenses melting under her attention. Adrian and I did our parts by staying quiet as much as possible.

"Why did you come to Virginia? I was under the impression you were working at the school," Mom asked.

"Oh, I am. I'm part of the alumni association. But that doesn't take all my time. We meet again next week. Since I had a few days, I thought I'd check on Adrian, make sure he was staying out of trouble." Allison gave Adrian an affectionate smile, as if saying she knew he wasn't causing trouble.

"He asked Violet to be his girlfriend. In a carriage! It was so romantic," Rose sighed.

I tried not to wince. Mom and Dad looked very stressed.

"I heard. Personally, I'm glad. Excited too. Violet's good for him." Allison grinned before stage-whispering to Rose, "Maybe we'll make a gentleman of him yet."

Adrian snorted, then gave Allison an innocent look when she looked at him.

"So you don't mind Violet and Adrian dating?" Rose asked.

"Me? I'm thrilled."

"Do you think your parents will object?" Mom asked. "After all, from my understanding, they've never met her."

Allison took a sip of water before putting down her cup. "I'm not sure. I think there are things they will like a lot about Violet. There are also a few things they probably won't be thrilled about. But most of those are the same things they are upset about with Adrian, so I don't feel the need to worry about it right now."

"Like what?" Rose asked.

Allison tapped her fork. "Well, I think our parents, Dad especially, expected Adrian to follow the same career that both he and his father had. Adrian is, no offence," she turned to Adrian who nodded, "both poorly suited and uninterested in that career. Violet isn't going to encourage him to follow that path, and Violet, again, no offense, I'm not sure you'd make a good politician's wife."

"None taken. I don't particularly want to be one." I suppressed a shiver.

"Wife?" Rose asked.

"Yes, isn't that a little presumptuous?" Dad asked.

Allison shrugged. "Perhaps. I'm sure neither of them are going to rush into things. But I also know that our parents would try to judge Adrian's girlfriends by whether or not they would make the model wife."

That earned me a few looks. "I'm not interested in getting married before I finish school."

"Good plan," Adrian said.

That might have been the best thing he said all night. It certainly helped my parents relax.

***

Everyone was sorry when Allison had to go back to Hyde. Having her around made everything smoother. But she couldn't stay for long. Before she left, Adrian announced that he had managed to get into the first summer intensive session, so he'd be leaving in about a week. In private, he told me that he hadn't actually gotten in, but he was going back to Wollaston Lake.

"My being here is just making everything harder for you. I know you're uncomfortable with this tension. I can come back if I'm needed." He rubbed his heart. He'd feel it if I were in danger. "I'll miss you, but I think…"

"No, you're probably right. Thank you for being so understanding. I'm sorry everyone's being…" Rose kept pestering him with intrusive questions, and Mom and Dad were just shy of rude. I suspected that when I wasn't around, they still played the 'wrong number' game occasionally. Or at least said I wasn't home.

"I think I understand."

I huffed. "Maybe you can explain it to me."

"It's pretty simple. But you won't like it."

No, I probably wouldn't. "Tell me anyway?"

"You changed since going to Hyde, right?"

"Undoubtedly."

"More than most people do when they go to college, and in ways your family doesn't appreciate." I nodded. Accurate so far. "But they love you, and always will. So they are trying not to alienate you. But then this strange boy comes, who may be a threat to their precious daughter…"

I winced. "And they take it all out on you. I'm so sorry."

Adrian shrugged. "They may not even be aware they're doing it. It's fine. Not the first time I've faced a hostile audience, won't be the last; and more deserved than some."

"Still, it's just…"

"It's just that you have different perspectives. Very different. They can't understand your side of your story. So you have to remember why they are acting the way they are. And that it's out of love."

"I know. I remind myself again and again. I'm still irritated, though. Sometimes," I admitted.

"I understand. But…" Adrian sighed. "Your family loves you. They may not appreciate what happened to you, or how you've changed; but they still love you. That won't change."

In other words, I shouldn't be complaining. "I know. I love them too. Even when they drive me crazy."

"That's what family is for."

I laughed at that. "I'll miss you. See you in July."

"I'll miss you too. Be careful. There may be a

security detail on you, I don't know."

"Doubt they'll bother. Not once you're gone."

"Don't know. The deal is that I don't have one while at Hyde. Technically, I'll be at Wollaston Lake, but that may be close enough. Ed, at least, knows," he made some vague hand gestures, "a lot. He might choose to stay with you, keep an eye on you."

"I don't think he likes me much."

"Oh, he likes you fine. It's all in how he hasn't kidnapped you again."

I snickered. "I'll keep that in mind."

Adrian scuffed at the ground. "I have to go. Enjoy your time with your family. Try to get along with them if you can. Call whenever you want. Be careful."

"You too."

He gave me a hug and a gentle kiss. It would be about six weeks before I saw him again. Longest time apart since we met. It was going to be a long summer.

Chapter Eight

The Forced Ally Moves

It was scary how going back to Hyde felt like more of a relief than going home did. Especially considering how no one had tried to kill me at home. Or frame me for major crimes, attack my friends, etc. This was probably not a good sign. Oh well.

I was going back to take Chemistry I as part of the second summer intensive. Adrian had a summer intensive too, I think in Biochemistry, but it might have been Organic Chemistry. Allison would be back and forth a lot. No one else would be here until the official semester started. Which apparently included Phyna, my new roommate.

Getting to Hyde wasn't difficult. Yes, I was tired and jetlagged, like usual. But Paul Rutchkin, the post master, once again offered to give me a ride to the ferry. Like he had when I came the first time. The ferry was running, since the ice had melted last month. Adrian was waiting at the dock when I disembarked, and helped me take my luggage to Addams.

Addams was more centrally located than Price, which had been close to the docks. It was one of two dorms, the other being Meyers, that was built with the creek running through the actual building, supposedly providing resources and living space for aquatic and semi-aquatic residents.

"Are you moved in already?" I asked, wondering

when Adrian came back to Hyde.

"Yeah, I've been here a couple days. Your old student pass will get you around for twenty-four hours, but you have to check-in to get anywhere after that. Best to do that before your pass expires."

"Okay, I'll go tomorrow when I'm slightly less brain dead." A good night's sleep would do wonders for me.

The RA on duty in my dorm was a pixie. Green and purple butterfly wings, about one and a half feet tall, blue hair. Differentiated from fairies by height, fairies were usually two to three feet tall; wings, fairy wings weren't as colorful, and were less obviously butterfly shaped; and the eyes. Pixies have triangular shaped pupils, while fairies often had slitted pupils. The rivalry between fairies and pixies was fierce enough that it was important to tell the difference at a glance. Having one of each on the floor last year had helped. Except when I got caught in the middle of one of their spell duels.

"I'm Merina. Fourth floor RA," she introduced herself.

"Violet Peters." I gave the nod-bow common in pixie greetings. Merina smiled in approval.

"You are in 108. Here's your key. Your RA is Clindoque. She won't be here for another week, so you can call me if you have any problems before then. My number will be on a board by your RA's door. Your key will open that door." Merina pointed to a door to the side. "All the rooms are down there. You, Sir, cannot go back there. No, not even to help the lady with her luggage. But you can wait in the lobby."

I didn't have much with me, since half my stuff was actually in Allison's room. Speaking of Allison, I hoped she was here. I asked.

"No, but she will be in a few hours. Why?"

"She has all my sheets."

Adrian chuckled. "Well, if she doesn't get back in time, I can probably lend you a set. I've got a Pink Panther set I've never used. Still in the plastic."

"I can only imagine. Allison?"

"Yeah. Can you take everything in one trip?"

I looked at my luggage. One suitcase and a backpack. "Yeah, I'm fine."

"I'll let you settle in, then. Meet you for dinner? What time?"

"It's six-forty?" I checked my watch.

"Four-forty. Remember, you moved back two time zones."

"I knew that. Seven?" I'd have to fix my watch, preferably tonight.

"Sure. I'll meet you here. Well, probably outside the dorm."

Right, back to school, back to danger. Adrian took his leave and I went to explore my new temporary home. The floor was quiet. I wondered how many people were here.

108 was near the end of the hall, because it was a shorter hallway than the rest of the floors. The set up was similar to my room in Price. The same gray carpet with white and black flecks. The same couch, a couple chairs, a desk with a computer, a sink, some counters and three doors. One had Phyna's name on it, one had mine, and one was the bathroom. If I wasn't mistaken, it was a little smaller than my room at Price. There was a window in the sitting room, but none in my room itself. Other than that, it was near identical. "Well, Violet, welcome home."

***

It was weird having only one class to focus on. Weird, but not necessarily bad. Having the suite to myself was weirder. At home, I had my own room, but the walls were far from soundproofed. Even before my hearing became slightly enhanced as a side effect of the oath, I still heard most of what happened in the house. At Hyde, other than the week or so I was at school over Christmas break, I had shared the suite with Ilse. Ilse was generally a quiet roommate, and we had different sleep schedules meaning we usually didn't overlap by more than four or five hours a day, if that. But even when she was asleep, there was a sense of presence that made the room not feel so empty.

At the moment, there was barely anyone on my floor, let alone my room. Of the ten rooms, nine of them meant for two people, there were two people present, including me. Three when the RA arrived the next week.

Clindoque was a centaur. Black fur and dark skin. She was more hands on than Thylica had been. Or maybe she was just more social. Either way, she made plans to eat at least one meal with each of her 'girls', as she called us, at least in my language, a month.

The two of us, an earth elemental and me, were, of course, first. Actually, I think I ate at least two meals a week with her before the main semester started.

First floor was usually assigned to beings who are ground based, have earth based powers, or have difficulty with heights. Hence why my RA was a centaur. I had no idea why Phyna was there, she's a flyer. They usually have top floor rooms. Once again I was glad I wasn't on the committee to design the school.

About three days before classes started, I was in the sitting room, reading one of the textbooks for my new classes, when I heard a key in the lock. The noise made me jump and stare at the door.

As soon as the door opened and I saw my dragon suitemate, I felt dumb for feeling startled. Of course, Phyna would be showing up about now. "Hello, Phyna. How was your summer?"

Phyna looked even more surprised to see me than I was to see here. "Could have been worse. How was yours?"

"About the same." I gave Phyna another look. While far from an expert on dragon health, she seemed frayed. "Are you okay?"

"Yes. It was just a little… much. You're back early."

"Yeah, I had a summer intensive. Chemistry I."

"Ah, so you've been here a while."

"Yup. All moved in." Phyna was moving very slowly. Almost as if she were in pain. Or possibly exhausted. Since it takes a lot to hurt a dragon, hopefully she was only tired. "Do you need to catch a nap or something? I mean, I know I'm always extremely out of it when I travel to and from Hyde. It's quite a distance."

Phyna nodded. "Might not be a bad idea."

"Well, don't stand on ceremony on my account. I'm just doing a little pre-studying, so I'll be quiet."

"Maybe I'll take you up on that. Sorry about being… unsocial."

I waved it off. "We've got a school year to become better friends. And it will be easier if we're both well-rested. Get some sleep."

She smiled, teeth displayed briefly, and I helped her take her luggage to her room. Apparently it wasn't my imagination about my room being smaller than my last one. Phyna's was noticeably bigger. Probably because Phyna was eleven feet long and between five and six feet high when she 'stood' normally. Then there were the wings. She needed the extra room.

While Phyna got settled in her room, I went back to studying, only to jump almost out of my skin when the phone rang a few minutes later. I grabbed it as quickly as I could before it disturbed her more.

"Hello?"

"Hi, Violet. It's Allison. I thought you would like to know that Ilse will be arriving tonight. So will Kara. Tim and the Ice Twins are expected early tomorrow, and Denise, late tomorrow."

"Oh, great. It will be good to see everyone." We had written, but I haven't seen any of them but the Chars since April. It was August now.

"Dinner tonight at eleven? Ilse and Kara will be there."

"Love to."

I felt the slightest hint of guilt as I hung up. I should be trying to make friends with Phyna. She was my roommate now. But I could work on becoming good friends with here later. It didn't negate my friendship with our group, or the fact that we had a job to do.

Maybe Phyna could be included. She probably didn't want the school to close either. Of course, therein lay the problem. 'Probably'. I didn't know her well enough to be sure.

Time passed, as it does. I passed Chemistry I with flying colors, much to my relief. Part of that was Adrian's help. Give me Biology any day. The school filled up with new and returning students, making it seem less like a ghost town, but increasing the odds of potential threats.

My friends returned, to my relief and pleasure. We had all missed each other, mostly, and made sure to have dinner to catch up and exchange room information and phone numbers. Tim and Adrian were both in Meyer, same floor even. "Good. You can watch out for each other," I said. It was better than having them share a room, which wouldn't have worked.

What was surprising, and perhaps a little alarming, was that other than Allison, who was in alumni housing, and me in Addams; all the other girls were in Stoker. None of them were on the same floor, other than Krystal and Bria, of course.

"Why am I the only one in Addams? That doesn't seem like a coincidence."

"It's not," Allison said immediately. "I don't know why, or who arranged it; but I am positive that isn't a coincidence. You were deliberately isolated."

Oh, yeah. It had been long enough since someone had targeted me that I had begun to feel left out. I was careful not to say that. Doubtful anyone wanted to hear my pessimistic sarcasm. "Well, it could be worse. Phyna isn't bad as a roommate. And she knows a lot about the library and the school."

"Do you know what type of dragon Phyna is?" Kara asked.

"No, I don't." One of the groups that might have

claim to the island if the school wasn't here was a dragon clan. Frostfire, if I remembered correctly. "I'll see if I can find a way to find out discretely." Some beings demanded more privacy than others. If Phyna was part of the Frostfire clan, then maybe she would know if there was a movement to take back the land. Not that she would necessarily tell me if there was, but then again, she might.

"Do be careful. You don't know her well, and it wouldn't be the first time that an enemy seemed a friend to your face." Adrian didn't look at me as he gave the warning. Then again, he had nearly been killed last time that happened.

"I'll do my best."

***

I had expected classes to get harder as I progressed through the years, really, I had. I simply had to remind myself of that fact sometimes. Like when, not even a month into school, I had three ten page papers due in the same week, a major exam in music, and a zoology lab that was worth a quarter of my grade in the same day. Sometimes, even staying organized and on top of things only helped so much.

As a result, I had taken to haunting the library. A lot. I worked better there. It was like a signal to my brain telling me that I needed to concentrate. Besides, Phyna wasn't nocturnal like Ilse was, so she was around more during the day. Dragon etiquette said one should pay attention to people around, which made studying a little awkward without one or the other of us feeling rude. Besides, I loved libraries. A pity this one had such huge drawbacks.

Not just the stone staircase that nearly killed me once, or the bookshelves that rearranged themselves when no one was looking, or even the classification system that I was beginning to suspect was invented by either tossing darts at a bunch of listed subject or pulling things out of a hat. There was also Ms. Grazletz, who was the dragon equivalent of every strict librarian stereotype, at least towards me.

Phyna was actually related to Ms. Grazletz, something like fourth cousins, twice removed, or something. That didn't sound close by human standards, but to dragons it was a much bigger deal. Phyna had shown me how to use the self-updating map and refine the catalog searches, but she couldn't help me with the classification system. We simply didn't have enough of a common frame of reference.

I was surrounded by books when I heard a familiar voice, "Long time, no see." Adrian was standing over me with a small smile.

"Sorry. Really, really, incredibly busy lately."

"Yeah, I remember."

Okay, maybe I had ranted about my workload a little bit. "You're a year ahead of me. How come you aren't buried in work?"

"I've been taking classes over summers and Christmases. Got a lot of my work intensive classes out of the way already. I'm only taking twelve credits. You have what, seventeen? With the labs?"

"Ugh, don't remind me."

Adrian shook his head with a smirk. "Anyway, I was looking for you. I have to go over to the mainland, I figured I'd ask if you wanted to come too. You look like you could use a break. Before your blood turns to ink and the librarians have to figure out how to shelf you."

I snickered. He had a point though. I'd been here at least two hours, today. It wasn't Saturday, his normal day to go entertain the local kids. "Would it be incredibly rude of me to ask why you're going to the mainland?" I stood, cracking my neck.

"Allison's birthday is coming up. I need to go shopping. There may not be that many choices in Wollaston Lake, but there's even less here."

"I didn't know Allison's birthday was soon. When is it?"

"Twenty-fifth."

I added the date to my mental calendar. "Sure. Maybe you can help me pick out something for her too."

"Then we better go. Ferry leaves in fifteen minutes."

I packed up my bags, putting my books on the 'to be re-shelved' rack. I'd put them away myself if I could understand the system.

Waiting for the ferry, I was struck by inspiration. Hoping it wasn't a terrible idea, I went with it. "So, you're from Toronto, right? Tell me about it."

Adrian looked at me blankly. "Well, you've seen Newport News, now. And Colonial Williamsburg, Jamestown, and didn't you see Yorktown? But I've never seen Toronto. So what do you like about Toronto, what don't you like?"

He shrugged. "Toronto is a big city. One of the major cities in Canada. Has a bit of a reputation for being greedy of resources. While we aren't historic like Colonial Williamsburg, there is a concentrated effort to keep the city from becoming too 'modern'. We still have street cars and are quite proud of them. Recently, an appeal to build a Wal-Mart in the city got turned down. There aren't any there."

Considering there were at least three Wal-Marts within twenty minutes of my house, I found that one hard to imagine. The ferry arrived then, and we embarked. "What else?"

"Toronto is one of the most ethnically diverse cities in our dimension. If something happened, making 13A no longer a shade dimension, I'm betting Toronto would take it pretty much in stride." I smiled at that. "Hockey is big. Very big. The Toronto Maple Leafs. They are my team, and heaven help anyone who naysays them."

I held up my hands. "I'm not criticizing them."

"Do you know anything about them?"

"Not a thing."

Adrian snickered. "How about any other hockey teams?"

"Not really. I've never seen a hockey game."

"That's okay. We can fix that."

It didn't seem a wise thing to say that I didn't care enough to fix that. Ah well, couldn't hurt to give it a try.

When we got to Wollaston Lake, we wandered around the town trying to find something Allison might like that we could afford and she wouldn't already have. I was in school on scholarship, discretionary spending was limited. I had never asked Adrian what his deal was, but even if his family was well off, if his relationship with his parents was so antagonistic, they might not be giving him more than needed to pay for school. Or they might. I simply didn't know.

I settled on a necklace of a bronze raptor in flight. It was probably a hawk, but I was going to say it was a kestrel. Adrian did not laugh at me when I said that, so hopefully it wasn't completely ridiculous. He seemed to think she'd like it, anyway.

Adrian got her a Tweety hooded sweatshirt, called 'bunny hugs' here, which I thought was absolutely adorable. He also ordered a fancy personalized cake that he'd have to come back and pick up in a couple days. Which worked out because this way, Allison wouldn't see it early.

Then we dallied, having ice cream floats at the general store, admiring flowers that were almost on their last legs, etc. Winter came early this far up north. Adrian shared a few Chemistry mnemonics he had acquired or created. We barely caught the last ferry back to school. I felt refreshed and ready to tackle my work again.

Allison was waiting for us on the dock. Adrian stiffened the moment he saw her. "Something's wrong."

"Yeah, I think I agree."

We were probably five minutes from docking, but Allison didn't want to wait any longer. She changed to kestrel form and swooped towards us, landing as human at our feet. The ferryman grumbled, but everyone else ignored it.

"Allison, what's wrong?" I asked. Somewhere in the back of my mind, I was thinking that it was a good thing I had the necklace in my pocket. An equally detached part of my brain wondered if she would have noticed if I was swinging it around a giant pink sign that said, 'LOOK WHAT I'VE GOT!'

"Something's wrong. Something's wrong and I don't know what. I just know it involves you. Something is really, really wrong."

Without thinking about it, I touched her shoulder, hoping to comfort, maybe help ground her. Instead, it focused her Sight. "The forced ally makes his move. You will have to choose between loyalties. Remember to ask the advisor for aid." Allison stepped back, away from me, shaking her head. "Wow. You… Look, you need to go home, okay? You have to answer the phone."

"O…kay." The word had about fifteen syllables when I finished. "I'll do that. Are *you* going to be okay?"

"Yes. Um, let me know what happens?"

"Sure. Well, if I have to answer the phone, I better get to my dorm." Good thing we were just pulling into the dock now.

Adrian walked me over, eyes darting everywhere; Allison following slightly, muttering to herself. I had seen Allison's visions before, but they never bothered her this long.

"Do you feel anything?" I whispered to Adrian.

"Something. But it's low level. Removed or far away."

I nodded as we got to Addams. "Okay, I'm going to stay here and work on my papers. I'll give you a call when I know what's up." I looked Adrian in eye and did a slight head tilt towards Allison. Basically asking him to look after her, and let me know if there was a problem. He nodded and shepherded her off.

When I got to my room, I gave a wary look to the phone, sitting there, looking innocent. Hopefully I hadn't missed whatever message I was supposed to get.

Since staring at the phone wouldn't make it ring faster, I tried to work on one of my papers. '*Tried*' being the operative word. I kept making stupid typos, forgetting what I was trying to say, and having to look up words I knew how to spell.

As time went on and the phone didn't ring, I got more and more apprehensive. Allison had been certain I need to be here and get a phone call. Hopefully one that would tell us who the forced ally was. To my knowledge, Allison's predictions happened. Period. End of discussion. But nothing was happening!

The longer I waited, the more my imagination ran away with me. I thought I had come up with almost every possibility that could be happening. I hadn't.

The phone rang, making me jump. Phyna wasn't here, so she didn't see me jump up, get my feet tangled in the chair and fall to the floor, get up, trip on the couch, and nearly brain myself on the table. I took a breath before answering it. Until I heard, I knew nothing. "Hello?" Silence. "Hello? Is anyone there?"

A sob. "Violet?"

"Mom?" I had to swallow bile, pain sharp in my stomach. What was going on? Why was Mom calling? What could make her cry like that?"

"Violet, I… You…"

"Mom, what's wrong?" More crying. "Are you alright? Dad? Rose?"

"We're fine. It's Jesse."

Jesse. The forced ally. The one who was on my

side by necessity, not because he wanted to be. How could I have been so *stupid*? "Jesse? What's wrong? Is he alright?"

"No! He's in a coma. The doctors don't know what's wrong with him, or if he'll ever wake up." The phone fell from my fingers, hitting the table with the thud of a death knell.

Chapter Nine

Oath Breaker

I did not *quite* barge into Taria's office, but it was a close thing. A very quick look around showed no one visible there but Taria, and it didn't feel like there was anyone invisible. Not a one hundred percent reliable method, but more accurate than one might think. "I need to go home. Family emergency."

If she was surprised by any of this, she didn't show it. Taria steepled her hands, and her wings, looking like sheets of snake skin, fluttered. "I suspected you might."

"What?" I was a closed mind. Taria couldn't read my mind at all. How would she know?

"Your cousin broke his oath. He attempted to tell someone about Hyde."

"What?" It was much quieter, more of a whisper or a gasp. My legs got me to her spare chair before deciding they weren't going to support me any longer. It should have been obvious. Forced ally makes his move. Jesse was in a coma. But hearing it...

"I do not know all the circumstances. What he hoped to accomplish, how willing he was, or what he planned to tell. I do not even know what happened to him. But I am made aware when students fall prey to the consequences of breaking their oath to the school."

"He's in a coma." Taria remained unmoved. I swallowed hard. These were questions I didn't want an answer to, but desperately had to know. "How long will he be in a coma? Will he be alright?"

"I do not know. The coma is not the consequence of his actions. Not the majority of the consequences, anyway. He is in a coma while magic judges him, based on the consequences set in the oath. He will be judged by his intentions, his awareness that he was breaking the oath, and the circumstances itself. It takes time for magic to judge these things."

"So, things could get worse?" I didn't want to hear this. I had to hear this.

"Your cousin violated his oath. That is a very serious charge." Taria all but sneered at the thought. "I do not know what will happen to your cousin. He may yet die." My vision whited out. "He may be fine once he wakes up. Most likely the consequences will be somewhere in between. He may end up with brain damage, or unable to talk, or missing memories. There is no way to tell before he wakes up."

"Can't you do anything?"

Taria didn't have eyebrows, but she somehow managed to raise one anyway. "You wish me to save one who would betray the school? No. Even if I wanted to, it is beyond my power. He is in magic's courtroom now."

It took three tries before I could swallow the rock in my throat enough to talk. "I still need to go home. For at least a week."

"Of course. He is kin, regardless of his actions. I will make arrangements for you with your professors. Have you travel arrangements?"

"Dad bought a ticket. I leave tomorrow morning. Early."

Taria nodded. "For your sake, I wish your cousin a fair recovery. But do recall, his actions are on his own head. Do not repeat them."

I left with unseeing eyes and shaky limbs. I had told the oath group, who were sympathetic, but none of them liked Jesse. Which, to be fair, was mostly Jesse's fault. But I didn't want to talk to them right now. I couldn't hear one more person talk about how this was probably Jesse's own fault, even if they were right. Maybe especially if they were right. I had told Clindoque, who had been fine with my leaving as soon as I mentioned a family emergency. There hadn't been time to tell Phyna, but I'd see her tonight. I didn't want to talk to my teachers about this, and schoolwork seemed so pointless. It wasn't until I wiped my face and felt water that I even realized I was crying.

"Are you alright?"

The voice startled me. I looked up to see a guy with messy dark hair. He looked familiar but I couldn't quite place him. "I will be, thanks."

He frowned. "Are you sure?"

I nodded, then squinted at him. Oh! "You! You're Nocht, aren't you?"

The guy blinked at me. "Yes? Wh... Oh, I remember you. Lavender?"

"Violet. Close enough. I never got the chance to thank you for your overview on the rules of magic last year, but it came in really, extremely handy." It had saved my life, actually.

"Oh, great! I love talking about magic." He gave me another look. "Hey, I know it's none of my business, but is there anything I can do to help?"

"No, I don't... Yes! Yes, you can. I need to know about oaths."

"Oaths?" Nocht blinked at me owlishly. "That will help?"

"Yes, it will. Do you know about oaths?"

"Well, sure."

"Great. Come on, I need some hot chocolate. I'll buy you one, and you can tell me what you know about oaths."

Nocht shrugged. "Okay."

On the way to the café, I managed to bring up a casual reference to my boyfriend, Adrian, just so Nocht didn't get the wrong idea, but other than that, I didn't mention my friends at all. "So, oaths."

"Okay, what do you want to know about them?"

"What happens if they get broken?"

"Depends. When an oath is written, the consequences are usually written in. A person who fails to do this will lose his hair, or who breaks this part will go blind, etc. That's why it's important to know exactly what you are swearing to before you swear. The consequences could be minor, major, or even lethal."

"What happens if the consequences aren't written in?" We hadn't said anything about what failure would mean when we swore our oath.

Nocht winced deeply. "Never, ever, *ever* agree to an oath like that. If the oath writer doesn't decide on the consequences, than magic itself will. And magic is like fire. Great in the right place, but always looking to break free. It can be a massively destructive force if you let it slip your control for a moment."

I swallowed hard. "Can the consequences be changed, added to, or subtracted from later?"

"No. Once an oath has been sworn, it's etched in stone. That is why you should never agree to an oath unless you know exactly what you are swearing to, that you can do it, and that you can trust the one who wrote the oath."

"How powerful are oaths?"

"Again, depends on the oath and the consequences written in. But a large part of it depends on the power of the participants. Okay, in court cases, people are 'under oath' to tell the truth, right?"

"Yes. But that's… It's not magic is it?"

"A little bit. It's not a very powerful oath, deliberately so. But it is an oath, and there are consequences for lying. Usually subtle ones that may not be immediately obvious. Sometimes they are never linked to the oath. But they are there. It's also weak because usually neither the person swearing nor the person asking the oath to be sworn have much in the way of magic. Also, it's sworn all the time. Magic simply isn't interested."

"So magic is more interested in unique oaths?"

"Seems to be. As much as magic has a personality. Though some oaths do get stronger because they've been around for a long time. Having different types of beings swear seems to make an oath stronger. Maybe it has to do with the different flavors of magic. For example, the oath of secrecy that the school puts on everyone when they come in is very, very strong because so many beings swear it every year. Many of whom have a lot of magic of their own which makes it even stronger."

"But not all realize what they are agreeing to. I mean, no one told me anything until I had been here almost an hour.

"True. If they could get everyone to *knowingly* agree, the oath would be even stronger."

I thought the oath was quite strong enough, thank you very much. Not only was I becoming more anxious about Jesse, I now had something else to tear my hair out over. "Why do some oaths become stronger over time, and others weaker?"

"Honestly, I'm not really sure. Some of it seems to be the amount of power in the oath originally, like if it was intended to affect heirs. Some of it is how many times it was broken. Every time an oath is broken, it's a little weaker. That's one of the reasons that *everyone* despises oath breakers."

I swallowed bile. "Right. Thanks, Nocht. I think you told me what I needed to know."

***

That night we met in one of the little side rooms in the second layer of the tunnels. It was one of the out of the way spots Adrian had found in his explorations, and could guarantee was seldom used. We had been using the library a lot, and we needed to change that up some. It didn't help that we were spread out among three dorms, four if you counted Allison's.

I reluctantly confessed what Taria had said about Jesse violating his oath, and tried to ignore the mutters of his foolishness. "It wasn't completely his fault. I knew these things could be fatal, but I never told him that. Only that it was dangerous and illegal." Why hadn't I told him? Why had I kept *that* a secret?

"Which was true. If he didn't believe what you did tell him, he likely wouldn't have believed you about their lethality."

I bit my lip. Snapping at Ilse would not help anything, and was undeserved. Probably.

"He probably won't die," Kara said. "These types

of oaths are severe, but death is a last resort."

"Okay, I can't talk about this anymore." I took a deep breath. "There's something else. Something we missed, perhaps because none of us are magical. We never set any boundaries for *our* oath. If my source is correct, that means that magic gets to decide the boundaries on its own. Since my force is a student I don't know well, we need to look into that."

"Yes, yes, we really do." Kara was white. Wasn't taking an oath her idea?

"We can look into that while you're back with your family," Allison said. "I hope your cousin is alright."

"Thank you. I've got to go. I'm leaving early tomorrow." And if I had to talk about this anymore, I was going to start screaming.

Adrian walked me back to my dorm. "Take care. Tell your cousin we wish him better." I nodded and promised to pass on the message, even if I knew it was only partly true.

Phyna was up when I reached my room. "Hey, you've been out all day. Is everything alright? Clindoque said something about you going away."

"Family emergency. My cousin is in the hospital. They… the doctor's don't know if he'll make it."

Phyna's tail whipped up to cover her mouth. "Oh, I'm so sorry. What happened?"

I wasn't going into this again. I couldn't. "The doctors aren't sure."

She bit the end of her tail, which probably hurt, before ducking into her room, calling over her non-existent shoulder for me to wait. A moment later, she scrambled back, tripping over her limbs. "I knew I had it." She held up an amber bracelet. "It's a good luck charm. For health and long life. You need it more than I do."

I still didn't believe in luck, good or bad, but I was touched. "Thank you. I'll give it back when I return."

Phyna shook her head. "No, it's yours now. It's bad luck to return a gift. Particularly a lucky gift. Wear it. Always."

It was a bad idea to argue with a dragon's generosity, anyway. "Thank you."

"When do you leave?"

"Tomorrow, early. Before breakfast."

"Then I may not see you again before you go. I wish you the best. Don't let anyone guilt you into coming back too soon. You stay as long as you need to. Or that you are needed." She wrapped her neck and tail around me briefly in the dragon equivalent of a hug, and I tried not to think about constrictors. "Get some sleep."

"I plan to. Thanks, again. I'll see you... when I see you." I went to my room, but sleep was slow in coming.

***

Sleep deprivation does not mean you can't be jittery with nervous energy, too. I was waiting for the ferry, wearing my backpack, the only luggage I was taking, and I couldn't stop fidgeting. Or talking. Adrian had offered to go with me to the airport, and seemed torn between resignation and amusement about my pointless chatter.

"I've got my jacket, just in case. Probably won't need it once I leave Wollaston Lake. Newport News is hot in August. Then again, airports can be cold. Tell Allison I'm sorry I have to miss her birthday."

"She knows. She's fine with it."

"I did give you the necklace for her, right?"

"Yes. But you can wait and give it to her yourself. She won't care that it's late."

I shrugged. I think it was a shrug. It may have been closer to a brief convulsion. "I think she should get it on time. That means something to a lot of people. I have my tickets and my passport, right?" I checked my pocket. "No, I have my passport and ticket number. The tickets are electronic."

"Well, they couldn't get you paper tickets so quickly."

"True." I was about to embark in another flurry of meaningless babbling, when someone called my name.

Taria approached us. "May I speak to you for a moment?" She looked at Adrian. "In private?"

Silently, Adrian sauntered a few feet away. He was still listening and we both knew it. Taria shook her head and muttered something I didn't catch, but evidently decided not to push it. "I thought a great deal about what you've said. I can do nothing to mitigate the consequences of your cousin's actions, and in honesty, might not even if I were capable. But there is one thing that is in my power." She held up a small round container of liquid. It reminded me of a tub of lip gloss. "This is *ritzayn*. I don't expect you to know the name, as it is extremely rare. If you can have your cousin swallow this, it will speed magic's judgement. It will not change the results, merely bring them on faster. If magic's judgement is that your cousin will stay in a coma until he dies, then he will die within a day or two. Otherwise, he will wake up, and you will know the results of his actions."

I swallowed hard, but didn't reach for the offered tub. "What's the price?"

"For you to have this ritzayn? Nothing. It is mine, and I freely give it to you. For your cousin if it is used? While he will wake from the coma, if to wake he is, in no more than a few days, his body will seem like it had been in one longer. As he is already in a hospital, I imagine they can solve any complications easily enough. Once more, let me stress, this *will not change the end result.* All it does is prevent you and your family from spending days, perhaps weeks, months, or years; waiting and wondering what will happen."

Slowly I reached out for it.

"The choice to use it or not is yours. If you do not, return it. If you do, return the tub."

"What if it kills him?" The question escaped me without my permission.

"Then he would have died anyway." It was said flatly, with no sympathy in her voice, but there was some kindness in her eyes.

"Right, thank you for the ritzayn."

Taria nodded. "Good travels to you. You can come back to the school at any time."

She turned and left, Adrian appearing at my side almost as soon as she was gone. "Do you think you'll use it?"

"I don't know. I just don't know."

"Not an easy choice. It really comes down to whether or not you trust Taria."

I hadn't thought of it that way, but he was right. Did I trust Taria? Could I trust her with Jesse's life?

***

Rose and Dad met me at the airport. "Your mother's at the hospital. Do you feel up to a visit tonight, or do you need to sleep, wait until tomorrow?" Dad asked.

"Any change?"

"None." Rose teared up.

"Quick trip."

I was exhausted, but my worry was stronger. "They might not let you in tonight," Dad warned me. "They are being very stingy with visits."

"I can try."

Mom, Uncle Jack, and Aunt Laura were at the hospital. Charlie was watching Leslie. At newly five, Leslie was too young to be here. Too young to understand.

"They're only letting in one person at a time, and only for ten minutes, an hour. You can go next," Mom said.

I thanked them, and sat down to wait. A loud silence filled the room, with no one wanting, or perhaps daring, to talk. After a few eternities, the doctor let in the next visitor. Everyone looked to me. I got up with a deep breath. Moment of truth time.

Jesse lay insensate on the hospital bed, looking gray. Different sensors were recording vital signs, and I had just enough training to understand most of them. Brain activity, thankfully, was steady. Not as strong as it ought to be, but present. Heart rate was slow, but he wasn't breathing through a ventilator, that was something. IVs in place.

A look at the chart had a lot of doctor language I didn't understand, and a few things I did. 'Coma of idiopathic origin'. That one I knew. Doctor speak for 'the heck if we know what's the matter with you'.

"Hey, Jesse. It's Violet." I took the chair by the bed, trying not to think of the tub in my pocket. Despite having thought of little else during the ten or so hour trip, I still didn't know what I was going to do. "I know you wanted me back from school, but there were other ways to do it." My voice broke as I tried to keep back a laugh. Or a sob. Honestly, I wasn't sure.

"Adrian says they all wish you well. To get better." Not even an eyelid flicker to hint that he could hear me. "Taria, my advisor, you remember her, wished you a... fair recovery, I think she said." There was silence except for the machines.

I let out a deep sigh. "Oh, Jesse. Why?" No answer. Should I use the ritzayn? Would it help? It wasn't just did I trust Taria, but did I trust Jesse? Did I trust that magic would find him innocent enough that this wouldn't kill him or damage him irrevocably? I had no idea.

Last time I had sat at someone's bedside while they were unconscious, someone else came in and tried to kill us. Therefore, I think I can be justified in being badly startled by the nurse who came and kicked me out. Still, I had been told ten minutes, and it had been about that, so it probably really was the nurse. To back that up, some of my family recognized her. Mom took me home, where I collapsed into bed.

Second day, same as the first. A little bit longer, and a little bit worse. No change in Jesse's condition and we spent most of the day in the waiting room, with him getting the occasional visitor. The doctors were trying to be reassuring, but I had enough medical training to recognize that they were skating by on fluff terms and didn't have a clue what was going on.

School hadn't started yet, so Rose and Charlie took turns waiting with us in the hospital and going home to watch Leslie. When Rose was at the hospital, she sat next to me, leaning on me, really. She was trying to read, but I doubted her efforts were any better than mine, and I couldn't remember a page after I finished it. About two, I offered to do a lunch run. Rose immediately jumped up to go with me.

It didn't take more than a minute to decide that the hospital cafeteria had absolutely nothing remotely appealing. "What do you think? Deli?" I asked.

"Yeah, sure."

I borrowed the car keys and requested everyone's lunch orders. There were a few 'whatever's. Not much in the way of definite answers.

Rose took a deep sigh as we pulled away from the hospital parking lot. I felt a corner of my mouth raise. "Glad to be out of there?"

"Yes! I mean, I know it's awful to feel this way. But just sitting there, not knowing, being bored; which is also horrible to feel. And worrying, of course I'm worrying–"

"Rose! Breathe. I understand. Trust me, I understand. I feel the same way." I felt the same way when Adrian got hurt, too.

"I didn't want to say anything in front of Uncle Jack or Aunt Laura."

"Probably a good idea. I won't either." I tried not to sigh. It wasn't right to ask Rose for more information. She probably didn't have any, and it wouldn't be fair to force her to go into it if she did. But maybe there was a way around that. "Do you want to talk about it?"

"No." She answered immediately, but it didn't seem accurate. I waited silently. "I was there."

"What?" Was she saying what I thought she was saying?

"When Jesse… fell. I was there. In the kitchen."

"I hadn't heard that. What… Can you tell me what happened?"

Rose stared out the window. "I was in the kitchen. Washing the dishes. Jesse came, and asked to talk to Mom and Dad. It seemed important."

"So you listened." I would have done the same.

"Yeah. They were both home, and they settled in the living room. Jesse said it was about you."

I was driving, had to pay attention. So I couldn't wince, but I wanted to. "What did he say?"

"He said they should get you to come home, quit Hyde. It wasn't good for you. Mom said you wouldn't agree to that. Dad pointed out that you were there on scholarship, so they couldn't even cut your funds to make you come home. Jesse said they didn't have the whole picture. I had finished the dishes, was walking towards the living room, when I saw him. He was so pale, and sweating. He said Hyde was… and then he was on the ground."

Jesse, you absolute moron! Why, oh, why did you have to speak up? Why now? This was intentional, deliberate. Magic was going to come down on him hard.

I pulled into the deli parking lot. "I'm sorry you saw that. It must have been really scary."

"Violet?"

"Yeah?"

"What was Jesse going to say?"

I closed my eyes and let out a breath. "I don't know." I started walking to the doors.

"But he was worried about you, about your school. What was he going to say?"

"I don't know, Rose. He didn't tell me he was going to do this." I would have told him not to.

She grabbed my arm. "Why did he say you had to leave?"

"Rose!" She was so pale. I gave her a hug. "I don't know what Jesse was going to say. Please don't ask me anymore." She shivered and deepened the hug.

"I won't." Her voice trembled. "But, if you tried to answer, would you be in the hospital too?"

Sharp kid. I tightened my grip on her. "Probably not." No, a deliberate violation, knowing what I knew? I'd probably be dead.

***

To my very great relief, Rose didn't bring up our conversation again. No one else had drawn the connection. Good, I didn't think Mom or Dad would back down on the subject. Rose had somehow gotten some hint that I *really* couldn't talk about some things. Maybe she had some deep instinctive belief in magic to fall back on. I don't think either Mom or Dad had that.

Hospital waiting rooms are awful places to be. In all fairness, people in hospital waiting rooms are usually sick, injured, dying, or waiting to hear about family or friends who are sick, injured, or dying. So it really doesn't matter how nice they made them, hospital waiting rooms would be miserable places.

It was Aunt Laura's third visit of the day, and she came out crying. Mom immediately led her to a quiet corner. The rest of us pretended we weren't here, and weren't listening. Actually, thanks to a side effect of the oath, my hearing had improved. Maybe I *was* the only one listening.

"I can't do this. I can't just keep waiting, never knowing. How long will he be like this? Why won't he get better? Knowing something, even the worst, would be better than this." Mom tried to comfort the sobbing woman, saying that at least he wasn't getting worse. "But he's not getting better, either. I can't stay in this limbo."

"I know. Waiting is the hardest part."

My throat was dry as if I had been swallowing corn starch. I could feel the tub of ritzayn in my pocket, as if it was on fire.

Two hours later, it was my turn to visit. I read his chart again, even though I probably wasn't supposed to. No change, doctors baffled. There was a nurse in the room, straightening things up.

I smiled at her, and tried not to look as nervous as I felt. In a way, I was actually glad she was there. As long as she was, I certainly couldn't give Jesse the ritzayn. I could put off my decision a little longer. Maybe long enough that Jesse would wake up on his own.

"Hey, Jesse. It's Violet again. We're all pretty worried. I'm told Leslie keeps crying that you aren't around." Or maybe it was that everyone kept leaving.

The nurse made a few notations on his chart. "You have another eight minutes. I'll come get you when it's over."

I nodded, any possible words dead in my throat. The nurse gave me a reassuring smile and left.

Slipping my hand in my pocket, I gripped the tub so hard that it hurt, leaving deep lines in my hand. The door was still open, and I couldn't shut it. I would have to be quiet. "Taria gave me something. It's…" I choked back a sob. "It might help. Or it might make things worse." A water droplet hit my shirt, then another. "I don't know. I don't know if I should give it to you. I don't know if it will help. I don't even know if you can hear me. Jesse, when you wake up, I am going to yell at you so much for putting us through this."

It was remembering what Aunt Laura said that tipped me over the edge. That even the worst was better than waiting and not knowing. There were small sponges on sticks that the doctors and nurses used to get him to swallow a little water. Even though he was getting nutrients through an IV, it was good for him to have some orally too.

After a quick check that no one was watching, I took an extra sponge, and dipped it in the ritzayn, which was, thankfully, colorless. The sponge absorbed it quickly, and when I put the sponge in his mouth and rubbed it around a little, automatic instincts kicked in, causing him to suck at the sponge. When he finished, I threw the sponge away in the 'biological wastes' container, took a regular sponge and gave him some water to cover up the ritzayn. Once he had that, I put the second sponge back in the water, and didn't touch them again. Especially since probably wasn't supposed to touch them in the first place.

I took Jesse's hand. "Don't make me regret that. Please, please don't make me regret that." I didn't say anything else until the nurse came. Then I left, praying I hadn't just killed my cousin.

Chapter Ten

Consequences

Dinner was a somber, near silent affair. Even thinking about eating made me feel vaguely nauseous. Actually eating didn't make the feeling worse, but it didn't make it better either. Nor was I the only one.

Rose was picking at her food, while I barely did that. Mom and Dad were eating, I think. My vision was a little blurry, making it hard to tell. I kept trying to distract myself, afraid that if I actually thought about the circumstances and what I had done, I would start screaming. I'm not sure I could stop if I started.

"Can I be excused?" Rose asked, possibly the first words spoken in the last half-hour. From the look of things, she might have managed to eat between a fourth and a fifth of her dinner. That still put her ahead of me.

"Me too?"

Mom sighed but nodded. "Wrap up your plates, in case you get hungry later."

We did, and disappeared into our respective rooms. The first thing I did was check my email. A distraction. I needed a distraction. Something to drown out the voice of doom echoing in my head. Email wasn't a help. Adrian, Ilse, and Kara each sent an email asking if I was alright because they were picking up on my emotions. Wonderful. I apologized for that, explaining that there was no change and I'd keep them posted. To

Adrian, I added a note saying I used Taria's gift. Nothing more than that.

A minute or so after I finished the last email and closed down the computer, there was a knock on the door. "Violet?"

"Come in, Rose."

She was wearing her pajamas and looked at me with red, tear-stained eyes. "I… I can't be alone right now."

I held out an arm and she collapsed next to me on the bed. "I don't want to be alone either."

"I'm trying not to think about it, but I just keep thinking, 'What if he dies'?"

"Me too." She had no idea how badly I agreed. Hopefully, she never would.

She found my wrist, with the amber bracelet. "Where did this come from?"

"A friend. She said it's for good luck, and I should wear it. Gave it to me when she heard about Jesse."

Rose traced over the square beads. "Do you think it works?"

I gave an abbreviated shrug. "Guess we'll find out."

"Thought you didn't believe in luck."

"I don't. But right now, I'll take what I can get."

We were quiet then. I think we even dozed off. When the phone rang, we both nearly jumped out of our skins. It was nearly eleven. There weren't too many good reasons for a phone call at this hour.

Rose and I crept to the door, opening it. Mom was talking on the phone. Couldn't make out what she was saying, but she sounded like she was crying. Stone. I was turning to stone.

Somehow, I was at the stairs as Mom finished the phone call, Rose hovering behind me. "Thank you for telling me."

She *was* crying. No, no, oh no. This wasn't supposed to be happening. Please, please, please don't let him be dead. *Please*.

"Mom?" Rose called, sounding as scared as I felt. I couldn't talk. I was too busy trying not to faint down the staircase.

Mom came to the base of the stairs, tears twinkling like stars on her cheeks and in her eyes. "You're awake?"

"Jesse? Is..." Rose couldn't ask either.

Then Mom smiled. Again, I nearly passed out. "He's awake."

***

We had been told there were complications, but no one was saying what those complications were. Not until we got to the hospital. Aunt Laura passed out hugs, crying as she did so. "He's awake, but seems to have had a reaction to one of the medicines. They are keeping him until that is solved."

"Reaction?" I asked.

"He's very malnourished, and the doctor's aren't sure why. But they are fixing it up." I couldn't tell if she was trying to reassure herself or us.

"No other complications?" I asked. That could have been a side effect of the ritzayn. What were the consequences?

Aunt Laura took a deep breath and gave a very unconvincing smile. "It's probably temporary, the doctors are hoping it is; but he's missing about a year's worth of memories. He doesn't remember anything after last September."

I collapsed on the closest seat, tears bursting free into heavy sobs. He didn't remember. He didn't remember Hyde, my friends or why he was so worried. *This was perfect!* He couldn't accidentally or deliberately betray the secrecy oath again. Jesse was safe.

"He'll be okay." Rose sat next to me, arm around my shoulders. "He'll get the memories back."

I truly doubted it.

***

Until the doctors either figured out what was going on, or Jesse was clearly much recovered, visiting hours remained unchanged. It was hours before I was able to see Jesse. That was okay. I needed time to think about what to say to him. My former plan to yell at him wouldn't work if he didn't remember what he did that made me mad. It wasn't enough time. A decade might not have been enough time. On the other hand, it was also too long.

Then it was my turn to see him. "He's still tired and very weak. He may fall asleep," the nurse warned me. "No more than ten minutes."

I nodded and think I said something agreeable before walking in the room. And stopping statue still.

"Violet, hi." Jesse smiled at me. I wouldn't have thought it possible for him to look worse conscious than he had in a coma, but he did. The gray tint was fading, but he looked skeletal. His fingernails were tinted blue, and his skin alternated between sagging and looking painfully stretched out.

My smile was pretty shaky as I walked in and sat down. "Hey, Jesse. You gave us all a scare."

"Sorry about that. Gave myself a scare too."

"Yeah, I bet." What did I even say to him?

Before I could, Jesse continued. "You started college, Hyde, right?"

"Right. Just started my second year."

Jesse shook his head, then leaned back, looking a little dizzy. "I can't believe I'm missing a year."

"Hey, we're all just grateful it wasn't worse."

He gave me a look. "No reassurances that I'll remember eventually?"

No, because I was willing to put money on him never remembering any of it, and I don't gamble. Instead I shrugged. "If you remember, you remember. But if you losing a year of memories is the price for getting you back safe and sound… Well, I'll take it. Of course, I'm also not the one missing memories."

"True. But I hadn't thought of it that way. So, do the doctors know what happened? They're being pretty vague to me."

"Same with us. But best I can tell, the doctors were pretty baffled."

Jesse looked away.

"Jesse?"

"What if I'm dying?"

My first instinct was to snap that he was *not* dying and to stop being ridiculous. Which might have made a little more sense than what I did say. "We're all dying. Of different things, at different rates. I'm a Bio major, remember? To live is to die. You had a close call, scared everyone. But however long you do have, don't waste it worrying about if you're dying."

Jesse gave me an impressed look. "Okay, then. No, you're right. But you'd tell me if I were in more immediate danger, wouldn't you?"

Would I? "To my knowledge, you are not."

"Thanks." Jesse smiled and the tension halved. "You learn that at that school of yours?"

"I don't know. Maybe?"

"You like it?"

"Yes, I do. A lot." Usually. He was going to ask now. I could tell.

Sure enough… "They said I went for a month and dropped out."

"You transferred. A better offer, I believe."

He scowled. "I don't remember any of it. At all."

'I wish I could just forget the whole thing.' "Don't worry about it. You really hated it there."

"Do you think I'll ever remember?"

Only if life was crueler than I believed it to be. "Well, if you do, call me. Right away. Day or night." Jesse laughed and I smiled back. "You think I'm joking. I'm not. Promise?"

He was still snickering. "Sure, promise."

Right now, he probably wouldn't remember this

conversation for very long. But if he did end up *remembering*, he'd at least understand why I said that. Hopefully he would contact me first.

The nurse came in and chased me out. I gave Jesse a quick, careful hug. "Seriously, don't go obsessing about this. And let me know if anything changes."

"I will."

That would have to be enough.

Chapter Eleven

Complications

Jesse was released from the hospital three days later, after the hospital managed to take care of all the complications of the coma and the ritzayn. The doctors were now confidently proclaiming there would be no permanent damage. I was reassured, but I know some of my family still had trouble getting past the fact that the doctors still had no idea what happened in the first place. Made it hard to trust them now.

While there was no permanent damage, Jesse was still fairly weak, and trying to readapt to the memories he had lost. They made arrangements with his current school for him to start over next semester. It had been a pretty awkward conversation.

The school had been informed when Jesse went into a coma, but were having more difficulty with the fact that he didn't remember applying to their school, let alone anything that happened last semester. Or the one before that, at a different school. He had taken classes and been graded for them, but now he didn't remember them at all. There was some debate on whether or not he should be retested, at least for the classes he took at his current school. Jesse was in favor of retesting, because he was Pre-Law, and would need that information. His parents weren't thrilled with the idea of having to pay for retesting or taking the classes twice. It hadn't been resolved by the time I was due to leave, but I was sure I'd hear ongoing updates.

Because Jesse was doing so well, I kept my original return ticket which actually had me leaving the day after Jesse went home from the hospital. I might have stayed longer, but it looked like the only thing that would help him now was time. Proving that he really didn't remember anything, Jesse was one of the people encouraging me to get back to school so I didn't fall behind in my studies. Which was another reason I was leaving. So far, I hadn't had any problems from the oath, but I didn't know how long my grace period would last.

One thing I had managed, was a quick visit to Linda Green, and I was still kicking myself for not talking to her before giving Jesse the ritzayn. Her explanation matched Taria's, at least. She was shocked I'd heard of it at all, and astonished that I had some to give to Jesse.

I was going to have to spend some more time looking into magic. My focus so far had been on the different races at Hyde. Fascinating information, and I could spend lifetimes studying it and still barely know a tenth of what was known. But I had the basics. Perhaps it was time to move on to a new subject.

My worst night was the last one. We had dinner at Uncle Jack and Aunt Laura's house, leaving early because Jesse still tired easily. I was about to head up to make sure I had everything packed, when Mom called me back.

"Yes, Mom?"

She hesitated. "Before… everything, Jesse came to talk to us." Rose looked up in alarm, biting her index finger. She hadn't done that in years. "He said it was important that you leave Hyde?"

I didn't say a word.

After a few minutes, Mom continued. "Do you know why he would say that?"

"No. He didn't tell me he was going to talk to you. I don't know what made him think that." Well, I didn't know what had been the catalyst. I knew why he thought that.

Dad cut in before Mom could say anything else. "You don't seem surprised."

"Rose overheard part of the conversation. She mentioned it to me. Also, I know Jesse didn't like Hyde, or the idea of me staying."

"But you don't know why?" Mom pressed.

"There have been a couple incidents." I shrugged. "I know he didn't adapt well. But I'm not sure why, and I don't know why he decided this now."

"Is there something you aren't telling us?" Dad asked.

Oh, lots. Lots and lots. "Nothing I can think of that would cause Jesse to suddenly declare I needed to leave." That sounded way too convoluted.

Mom frowned. "Violet, I don't want to say this; but I'm not sure you are being completely honest with us."

Because I wasn't. "I've told you as much as I can. I don't know what happened."

"What time does your flight leave?" Rose asked, obviously trying to change the subject.

I leapt on it. "Nine in the morning. I should be at the airport by seven."

"Can I go to the airport with you?"

"If you want to get up that early, it's fine with me."

Mom gave a soft huff. "Yes, Rose, you can go. But back to the subject at hand–"

"What time are we leaving?"

"Probably around six-thirty. But don't interrupt, Rose," Dad said.

"Exactly. Now, Violet–"

"I'm not sure what else I can say. I've told you what I can. I *don't know* what Jesse planned, and for now, he doesn't know either. I'm sorry you feel like I'm keeping secrets from you, but there is nothing more to say."

Mom opened her mouth to say something, but Rose jumped in first. "Since we have to get up so early, maybe we should go to bed."

"Good idea. I know I'm wiped." It was the day after full moon, I noticed. Thanks to the oath, Kara inadvertently borrowed energy from some of us every full moon. It wasn't the same people, none of us were as tired as she would be without it, and there was nothing she could do about it, so we didn't complain. Must be my turn. Or maybe not. I still hadn't recovered my emotional balance since Allison told me I had to go home and wait for a phone call. That wears you out, too.

"Perhaps that would be best." Dad sighed.

I think Mom wanted to argue, but changed her mind. We were all hurting when Christmas break was a disaster, and no one wanted a repeat.

It was still early, so I wasn't surprised that after getting ready for bed, I found myself lying there, sleep nowhere to be found, despite my weariness. After about an hour, there was a soft knock on the door. "Violet, are you awake?" Rose whispered.

"Yeah, come on in."

She was wearing the Hyde tee-shirt I gave her for her birthday last year. It was shorter now than it used to be. Idly I wondered if it had shrunk in the wash or if she had grown a little. Rose didn't seem any taller, I thought, but the lettering of the shirt had started to fade. "Can't sleep?" I asked

"No." She joined me on the bed, a stuffed wolf in one arm and a stuffed moose in the other. Pretty sure I gave her the moose too.

"Me neither."

"I just…"

"Wanted the conversation to be over. Wanted to avoid a fight. I understand, and appreciate it."

Rose lay down next to me, brown eyes catching the street lamp outside. "I didn't want anything to happen," she whispered. "I don't want you to end up like Jesse."

I could barely breathe. Rose knew. Not everything, I was sure. But enough. How? Right now, it didn't matter. "I'm not going to. Not if I can help it."

"Violet?"

"Yeah?"

"Why did you decide to go to Hyde anyway?"

"Well, they have an amazing genetics program. Absolutely astounding. I can't tell you how much I'm learning there." About so much more than genetics.

"Why did you decide to become a geneticist?"

I smiled. "Actually, it was partially because of you."

"Me?" Rose sat up, looking at me. I pulled her back down. "What did I do?"

"You didn't *do* anything. I remember, I must have been about seven, and I asked Mom how come I had blue eyes like her, and you had brown eyes, while Dad's are more hazel. Mom tried to explain a very basic version of genetics. I remember picturing it like a computer or slot machine that picks which trait each person gets. About a week or so later, there was a documentary on Mendel that Dad let me watch. After that…" After that, I had 'established an interest', so Mom and Dad, and eventually Rose, would sometimes get me things related to the subject. I think Uncle Jack and Aunt Laura encouraged it too. At twelve, I learned about the Human Genome Project, and decided I wanted to be involved in something like that.

Rose frowned, but didn't say anything for a long time. "How *do* I have brown eyes? I thought brown was dominant."

"It is. But there are six different traits that go into determining eye color. That's why there's so much variety. There's eight traits that go into determining hair color."

"Oh. Do you think if I had blue eyes like you, you still would have been interested?"

I gave a half shrug. "Maybe. I've always been curious. But I don't know if I would have latched onto genetics as my chosen career field if it hadn't been for my curiosity being encouraged and reinforced like that."

There was an even longer silence. I was almost asleep when I heard Rose mutter, "I knew there was a reason I always wished I had blue eyes like you."

***

I woke up the next morning with an unexplained weight on me and a sharp pain in my side. As I continued to wake up, I slowly realized that both the weight and pain had an explanation. Namely, Rose fell asleep in my bed and was currently spread out like she was trying to take up as much space as possible. One elbow was digging painfully into my side, her leg was on mine, her head pinned down my hair, and her arm was across me with her hand in my face. I moved the elbow and the hand, but left the rest for now.

Being very early morning, the room was dark. I had to grope around for my back lit alarm clock. Five-forty-five. Yuck. Still, I should get up. If I could get away from octopus Rose. She whined as I pulled away, but I managed, bit by bit. Before misjudging the edge of the bed and falling to the floor with a thud.

"Huh? What happened?" Rose looked around, no awareness behind her eyes.

"Nothing. If you're coming with me to the airport, you should probably get up now."

"But then what will the elephant do?"

For a moment, I considered trying to answer that, before deciding not to bother. "Either get up or go back to sleep."

Rose gave a decisive nod. "Fishies." Then she nuzzled back into my pillow.

I snickered, but dressed in the dark. She could sleep a little while longer. Mom exited her room as I was heading to the bathroom. "Oh, good. I was just checking to see if you were up."

"I am, but Rose is still asleep. She's in my room."

Mom looked puzzled. "Why is she asleep in your room?"

"She didn't want to be alone. Neither did I."

"Fair enough. I'm going to make breakfast. Make sure she wakes up?"

"Will do."

A few minutes later, I was back in my room. This time I turned on the light. Nothing. "Rose, time to get up." Nothing. I put an arm on either side of her and pushed the mattress up and down. She gave a mewling whine and pulled the covers over her head. "Oh, really?"

I collapsed on her. "Rosy-posy, time to wake up."

"Don't call me tha'."

"Why not, Rosy-posy? Rosy-posy the flower queen. Rosy-posy the–" The blankets attacked me, almost causing my second collision with the floor that morning. "Awake now?"

"What time is it?"

"Not yet six." Rose made a face. "Did you want to come to the airport or not?"

"I'm getting up. Just give me a minute."

"Mom's making breakfast." I scooped up my pajamas and deodorant, and tucked them both in my backpack, along with my toothbrush. That should be everything.

"What's for breakfast?"

"No idea. Let's find out. Get dressed." I slung my backpack on and headed downstairs. No point leaving it here, I probably wouldn't be back up.

Breakfast turned out to be French toast. It was quiet meal, probably because most of us were still half asleep. At least I could catch some more sleep on the various planes. There wasn't much else to do there.

"When do you start school?" I asked Rose. Pretty sure I should have known that already, but I couldn't remember.

"Next week. Which means I can sleep in tomorrow while you have to get up for classes."

"That's what you think. My earliest class is ten. And that's two hours behind here, so it's like noon." Only for a couple days, until I got used to it, but still.

Rose pouted. "Not fair."

I shrugged. "Way it goes." No one in my family is fond of mornings. No one.

"Is it going to cause problems, you leaving classes like that?" Rose asked.

"I cleared it with my advisor. She said that she'd handle my professors. She's one of them, and I've had most of the rest of them before; I think it'll be okay." Dr. Gronk was amazingly understanding. Ms. Shale was usually sympathetic. I had Dr. Rigor, a zombie, for Chem. I, and now again for Chem. II, and he barely seemed to care about attendance as long as we were careful about safety. Dr. Ashe, the dryad I had for botany, never took attendance. I should be fine.

"That nice Ms. Clay woman?" Mom asked.

Fortunately, I had just taken a large bite of French toast so I didn't ask her who she was talking about. Chewing as slowly as I could, I tried to figure out who she would be referring to. Oh! Right, Taria talked to them while calling herself 'Taria Clay'. I had forgotten that. "Yes, I have her for history."

"Good. I liked her." Dad looked at his watch. "Are we about ready to go?"

Rose and I gathered the dishes, pouring water over them to loosen food and syrup, then we headed out. Early morning traffic was calm. The airport was even quieter.

"Thank you for coming home." Mom gave me a big hug. "Be careful out there."

"You sure you can't stay any longer?" Rose asked.

We were at the airport. I was about to check in, ticket in hand. But at that moment, I choked. It was all I could do to not suddenly beg to stay longer. But no, I had to get back to Hyde. Classes, my friends, the oath. I had to leave. But if I spoke, I knew I'd say I'd stay longer. Crazy. Just plain crazy. Instead, I smiled and gave her a hug.

Dad was the one who pointed out I couldn't stay. "But she'll be back for Christmas. Right?"

"Of course. I'll probably even be back before Rose's birthday."

"You can come back anytime," Mom said. "If you want to change schools, just say the word. We'll help you research."

"Thank you. But I really think I'm where I'm supposed to be." There was a final round of hugs, and I checked in, moving to the gate.

At some point over the summer, they had upgraded security at the airport. There were scanners that can see through clothes, I could never remember the name of them. Part of me wanted to be upset by the intrusiveness of it, but honestly, Hyde's security measures were probably even more invasive, even if I didn't always realize when they were used. When I asked, I was told the scanners were put up in July. I must have missed it by a week or two at most. New security or not, it didn't take long to be cleared.

One and a half hours until I could board. One and a half hours where I steadily found myself feeling worse and worse. My stomach was churning, with bile trying to escape up my throat. Despite sitting down, my legs felt shaky, like they couldn't support me. My face was hot to the touch, and I was sweating. I could tell, because those parts were chilled in the cold airport. Twice, I was certain I was going to throw up. A few more times, I wished I would, because maybe I'd feel better afterwards.

Had something been wrong with the eggs in breakfast? Was this nerves? I couldn't understand it. I wasn't sick. No prior symptoms. But right now, I wanted nothing more than to curl up on this filthy airport rug and cry for Mom and Dad. Nerves. Had to be.

Was I picking up on someone else? I tried to separate and analyze the feelings. Nothing that suggested foreign emotions. As far as I could tell, this was me.

Had I somehow violated part of the oath? I couldn't think of how, unless it was mad I had skipped a week of classes. But I was heading back now.

At least three complete strangers asked me if I was alright. I smiled and said yes, praying that I got over this quickly and they didn't decide I was too sick to fly.

When they called my section to board, I stood up. My knees didn't get the message, and I ended up on the floor. A blond man, probably in his thirties, helped me stand. "Are you sure you're okay?"

"I'm fine. Really."

Unfortunately, the flight attendant checking boarding passes had seen me fall. "If you're sick–"

"I'm not. It's just been a really bad week."

She gave me a dubious look. "Please wait to the side. I want you checked by a medic."

Sighing, I took a seat. Luckily, small airport, someone was there in minutes. A woman, I'd say in her mid-forties. "So, you aren't feeling well?"

"It's nerves. I was fine two hours ago."

"Hmm." She pulled out a forehead strip and placed it against me to take my temperature. "Are you afraid of flying?"

"No."

"Have you flown before?"

"Yes. I'm going back to college. It takes a few planes to get there."

"Do you live in the area?"

"Yes. My cousin ended up in the hospital. I had to see him."

She went grave. "Anything contagious?"

"No, they called it an aneurism." Among a few other theories. "I think I'm just worried something else will happen if I leave." That made about as much sense as any other theory I had.

"Is he better now?"

"Out of the hospital."

"Well, you don't have a temperature." She tried a blood pressure cuff. "No talking." I didn't, but I did wince at the restricting band. "Blood pressure is a little low, but not in the danger zone. Pulse is elevated, but, again, not dangerously so."

I nodded.

"How's your throat?"

"Not sore."

"Dizziness?"

"Not anymore." Mostly.

"Well, I don't see any reason to prevent you from flying if you think you're up to it."

"I am. Thank you."

The flight attendant grudgingly let me on. I boarded the plane, barely hiding the sudden onset of dizziness. Once I was back at Hyde, I would be fine, wouldn't I? I found my seat, and it wasn't long before take out. I'm not sure what happened next, because I passed out before we leveled off.

Chapter Twelve

I'm fine, really.

I woke up to fingers on my neck. That made me jolt and smack them away. There was a man standing over me. Salt and pepper hair, wearing wire spectacles. "Feeling a little better?"

"What?"

"You passed out."

I blinked. Had I? Must have. "Yes, I'm fine now." And I was the center of attention. Grand. At least the plane hadn't landed, and didn't seem to be about to do so. "Sorry."

The doctor, I assume, walked me though most of the same steps as the medic at the airport. No, I didn't have a fever. Pulse and blood pressure were actually closer to normal. No, I hadn't been exposed to anything contagious. No, I didn't feel sick. Which was closer to the truth than when the medic asked. Still felt miserable, but not as bad.

Since I continued to argue that I was fine and the doctor couldn't find anything wrong with me, he changed seats with the woman I had been sitting next to, and asked the flight attendant to give me some crackers and water. They had pretzels instead. I ate them slowly, with the water, under the doctor's watchful eye.

When I finished, only doctor was still paying

attention to me. "Feeling better now?"

"Some. Sorry about that. I don't know what happened."

"Unfortunately, neither do I. That is not a normal reaction. Not without underlying causes."

No, it really wasn't. "I had a bad week. I think I'm running on fumes now."

"Is Chicago your last stop?"

"No. I have to take a plane to Saskatoon, and then another to Wollaston Lake."

He pushed his glasses back in place by the right corner. "That's too bad. I was going to recommend they look you over when you land."

"I feel better now. Lots." Well, comparatively. "And I really don't want to miss my connecting flights." That might add a little credence to the oath theory. If the oath could tell I was on my way back, it might reduce the consequences.

"Do you have a history of low blood pressure?"

"Not to my knowledge."

"Anxiety attacks?"

Yes, but that was completely different. "There was a brief time some months ago, but we figured out what was causing that. I haven't had one in ages." Of course, there was nothing saying it couldn't happen again, but it hadn't felt anything like this.

"Heart problems?"

"No. I played sports in high school. Yearly physicals. No heart or lung troubles."

The doctor took of his spectacles and cleaned them. "Then I'm not sure what the problem is."

"Psychosomatic. Part of me really doesn't want to leave home."

He laughed. "That may be. Do you normally have problems flying?"

"No. First time. And yes, I have flown before."

"Have you passed out recently?"

"No. In fact, I think this was the first time ever." No, second. But that was being forcibly knocked unconscious. That doesn't count. And it was almost a year ago.

"Did you give blood recently, or suffer an injury in which you lost a fair amount of blood?"

"Nope."

"Any changes in medication?"

"I don't take any regular medication. Never have."

"Then I really don't know what to tell you. But if

this happens again, I'm going to advise you to stop flying, at least until you figure out the cause."

That would be problematic. "Well, then it had better not happen again. Because it would take days to get back and forth between Wollaston Lake and Newport News if I had to drive."

"Where is Wollaston Lake?"

"North Saskatchewan. Really, really north Saskatchewan."

He chuckled at my apprehensive sounding talk. "North of the Arctic Circle?"

"No, but close. I have actually crossed into the Arctic Circle. A friend invited a group of us to meet his family." There was no way I was saying that I went to the North Pole.

"In the summer?"

"January. Yes, it was really, *really* cold."

"I imagine it was."

Landing went better than take off. I didn't even come close to passing out. There was more than an hour before my next flight, so I was given a quick examination. To my total un-surprise, they could find nothing wrong with me. Which did not stop them from passing on a message to the flight attendants to keep an eye on me.

Embarrassed but feeling better, I landed in Wollaston Lake with no more fainting spells. Comparatively, I felt much, much better. Tired, drained, and ready to sleep for a week, but I didn't feel sick.

Adrian met me at the airport. "How's your cousin?"

"He got home yesterday. Still doesn't remember anything about the past year."

"Probably never will."

"Yeah."

Adrian looked like he was trying to think of something comforting, but gave up. "Any luggage?"

"Nope. Only needed the backpack."

"Right. C'mon, if we hurry, we can catch the ferry."

I nodded and picked up the pace. It was probably the last ferry of the day. We did make it, but my energy was seriously flagging before we reached the island.

"Do you think you made the right choice?"

I brushed hair from my face. "About using Taria's gift? I think maybe I did. Maybe he'd be up by now without it, but maybe not. Of course, there's also the fact that the consequences seem to have been relatively minor. Had they been worse, if he had actually died... I might have a different answer."

Adrian gave a half nod. "We did some research. Because it's a *school*, lethal results were supposed to be a last resort. And only if he had true malice in mind, against the school, not you personally."

Would have been nice to know that *before* I gave him the ritzayn, but they might not have known then. In any case, I didn't have the energy for an argument. "Did you look into oaths?"

He scanned the area, as if to make sure we were truly alone. "Yes. Your source seems to be correct. Allison is trying to figure out what can be done, but we're getting nowhere fast."

Allison had been convinced our oath was a good thing. Kara had suggested it. But we all agreed to swear the oath. Every one of us. "Well, we can all help some."

"Yeah." The ferry reached the island and we disembarked. Adrian walked me back to my dorm. "We're all glad you're back."

I smiled and thanked him. There was no way I was going to mention how much of me wanted to run back home. If only I could figure out where that was.

***

Phyna looked up from her textbook as I half-stumbled into the room. "Oh, you're back! Already?"

"Yes, I'm back. I think."

She gave a draconic smile. How many teeth did

dragons have? "You're back. How's Jesse?"

"Better. He's out of the hospital. There were some complications, but I think he's going to be alright." I didn't want to go into what had happened and why. There was no need, and it certainly wouldn't help anything.

"Good. I'm glad. But why did you come back so soon? Shouldn't you have spent longer with your family? At least until your cousin heals from his injury?"

Should I have? "If he was still in the hospital, I probably would have. But he's getting better, stabilizing. I have classes. I figured it was time to come back."

Phyna gave a look that would probably be a confused frown on a human. "Cultural differences?" Wouldn't be the first time we had that problem. Dragon culture was very different from human culture. More so than vampire culture, and unlike Ilse, Phyna wasn't training to be an ambassador.

"Perhaps. I take it from your perspective I should have stayed?"

"Family needs family in difficult times." Was it my imagination or did she wince there?

"I did go home, and if there was anything I could do to help, or even if things were still uncertain, I would have stayed longer. But I can't do anything to help. Things are getting better. I didn't see a point, not as things are."

"I suppose," Phyna said, sounding like I was

trying to convince her that clouds were rocks, but she was too polite to argue with me over it.

My face itched, so I rubbed at it. I might not feel as bad as I had earlier, but I still wasn't sure that 'death warmed over' wouldn't be an improvement. "Would you consider it unforgivably rude of me to go lie down for a while? I... I'm not feeling quite up to par."

"No! By all means, rest." She eyed me up and down. "Do you need a healer?"

"No, just rest." I'd probably skip dinner. Despite not eating more than pretzels and other airplane snacks since breakfast, the idea of food just made me feel nauseous.

"Well, sleep well. Let me know if you need anything."

I gave her a friendly nod and went into my room. It was the same room I had left about a week ago. I was the same Violet. But it felt like one of us had changed. I didn't feel at home; I felt lost, displaced.

This wasn't the time. Feeling bad was making me maudlin. I was fine, Jesse was fine, and we were both back where we were supposed to be. Maybe I'd feel better if I rested for a while. I lay down on the bed, closed my eyes, and didn't wake up again until morning.

***

My first class was history with Taria. Sleep had helped. I was able to eat, and most of my symptoms seemed to be over, but I was a little shaky still. Must have been a stomach bug, exacerbated by flying. Or it was the oath and it was satisfied by the fact I was back.

I stuck around after class, waiting until everyone else had left. When we were alone in the classroom, I walked down to her desk and handed over the empty tub of ritzayn. "Thank you."

She took it gravely. "So you did use it. I wondered. Did it help?"

"I think so. He woke up a few hours after I used it." Felt like forever at the time, but it was actually less than six hours.

"Good. He is… well?"

I had wondered if she would know the consequences. "He doesn't remember the past year. Other than that, he seems fine."

Purple wings arched and spread out like a bat. "I see. Your cousin is uncommonly lucky. I would have expected something more severe."

Somehow, I choked back my first, second, and third responses to that. Mostly a mix of rage and horror. "Well, personally, I'm glad it wasn't."

"Quite. Did you have any issues or questions over what was covered?"

"Actually, yes. I was a little confused over the trial of Trisix, the goblin outlaw. Why was the first trial considered invalid?"

"Because Trisix, due to sabotage, ended up delirious when sentencing was pronounced. It is a basis of Interdimensional Law that the accused be present and aware at the time of the sentencing."

"Huh. I know that in my dimension there is a foundation to try someone when they aren't there. It's called *in absentia*. I don't know the requirements, and it isn't done often, but it can be done."

"That may work in your dimension, but any interdimensional court, including here, follow Interdimensional Standards. That would not be possible."

I took a few quick notes. "Well, that explains that. Thanks."

"Of course. Were there any other issues?"

"Not about history. Thank you for clearing my absence with the other professors."

"By all means. They were happy to give you the time you need. Is this your first class since coming back?"

"Yes. I got back late yesterday."

Taria folded her hands as her wings shifted again, more dragonfly this time. "Are you well? You seem a little off."

"Stomach bug, I think. I felt awful yesterday, but

I'm better now."

"Good. Do remember that we have an excellent medical facility."

That was painted in a truly painful combination of colors. "Yes, I remember. I'd better go."

"Of course. Remember to see me if there are any issues."

***

Readjusting to Hyde was harder than it ought to have been. I was only gone a week, it wasn't like I had forgotten how things worked. Yes, there was the work I had to catch up on, and thank goodness that I was only gone a week within a month of school starting. The teachers were being very understanding in giving me time to do the make-up work. Then there was the typical adjustment of reality I had to do every time I left or came back to Hyde. But what surprised me was how difficult it was to get into the swing of things.

I had less energy than I was used to, and was moodier. Sometimes just getting up seemed like a Herculean effort. Catching up with school work was actually painful. I had trouble focusing, got distracted easily, and really didn't want to study. The headache I had every night for a week didn't help. But I had to push through it or I would be in violation of my oath, and risked losing my scholarship. Part of me wondered if that would be a bad thing.

Trudging my way back to my dorm from class, I

was intercepted by an enthusiastic missile. "Hey, Violet! Allison brought some Pink Panther cartoons from home. We're going to watch them on her laptop. You in?" Kara bounded around me, her very exuberance draining me, as if she was stealing my energy for herself.

"When?"

"Right now."

I didn't want to. I wanted to go home, take some aspirin or something, and maybe finish my paper on how the elephants of 13A might be related to the *gesuati* of 11B. Probably make it an early night. I didn't want to talk or hang out. Noises bothered me more, overwhelming me when there were too many. Sleep was becoming more difficult, so I was snappish. But I also hadn't spent much time with my friends lately. "Okay, for a little bit. I don't know how long I can stay."

"Great! Come on, come on." She loped off.

I shambled after her. Library, huh? That made sense, I guess. We could borrow one of the study rooms. Enough room, and outlets. For all dimensions.

Everyone seemed pleased and surprised to see me. Had I really withdrawn that much in the two weeks I'd been back? Maybe I had. Something else to work on. There was so much to work on right now. It was like quicksand dragging me down.

"Glad you could join us." Allison beamed widely. "All caught up?"

"Pretty much. Now I have to work on staying that way."

Allison started the cartoons. It took about a half-hour for me to notice a problem. Pink Panther cartoons are supposed to be funny. Even Tim, who had the least background knowledge to understand them, found certain parts funny. Even Ilse, who was the most reluctant to show emotion in public, was willing to laugh here. I didn't laugh. Didn't even crack a smile. Not once.

After another fifteen minutes, I clearly wasn't the only one who had noticed. "Are you okay?" Denise asked.

"Fine."

"You don't seem to be enjoying the pictures," Ilse ventured.

"They're fine."

"So, what's wrong?" Adrian asked.

"Nothing. I'm just tired."

"I thought humans often laughed easier when tired. You keep saying that," Kara said.

I shrugged. "Guess I'm just not in the mood. Don't let me ruin it for the rest of you."

"If you'd rather do something else…" Allison asked.

"No, not really. This is fine." There wasn't

anything I wanted to do.

Adrian put a hand to my forehead. I jerked away. "I'm not sick."

"You sure?"

"I'm fine."

"You've been acting... out of character, for a little while now. Perhaps it would not be ill-advised to allow yourself to be seen to at the infirmary?" Tim suggested hesitantly.

"I'm fine."

"When's the last time you laughed?" Adrian asked

"I'm *fine*! Would you just drop it, already?" I took a deep breath. Shouting wasn't going to help anything. "Really. I'm fine. I didn't sleep well last night. I think I should make it an early night. Enjoy the cartoons." Now I had to extricate myself from the middle of the group without disrupting everyone.

The same everyone who were still staring at me. Probably because I didn't go around yelling at people that often. "Sorry. I didn't mean to snap like that. Can I leave now?"

"Um." Krystal raised a tentative hand. "I actually had a question for you. Not related to your health."

Another deep breath. No lashing out at people

who didn't deserve it. Krystal, at least at the moment, didn't deserve it. "Yes?"

"I'm supposed to read this book from your dimension. *1984* by George Orville."

"Sure, I read that in high school." Didn't like it much, but I had read it.

"This is a history text?"

"What? No! No, *1984* is fictional. It was actually written in 1948 and he transposed the numbers. There are a few element that are true, or came close to coming true, but the book is fiction. The government cannot watch us through our televisions, people do not get arrested for their thoughts. Well, not in most countries. There are some really strict dictatorships, but only a few. I think. And the government does not have video recordings and listening devices everywhere." That also needed a little clarification. "Though that one came closer than some. There are cameras in lots of places, most people use traceable cards to make purchases, and internet usage can be tracked. But they need a warrant for that. In most countries."

Kara shook her head. "That's a lot of control."

"Yeah, some people are pretty worried about it, but most ignore it since it doesn't affect their daily life. Of course, private citizens can get a hold of spy cameras and listening devices too, if they know where to look."

Ilse sat up straighter. "These devices do exist? Like in that movie you showed me? And they can be hidden?" I had shown Ilse a spy movie once. Didn't remember which one, but I had pointed out that not all of it was real. I suppose I should have been more specific about what was and wasn't real.

"Certainly. I mean, they can make cameras smaller than a pencil eraser. I think listening devices can be even smaller. Ilse, what's wrong?"

"I had a thought." She scanned the room as if analyzing every cranny.

"Care to share with the rest of us?" Adrian asked, leaning back on his chair.

"No. Not yet. I need to confer to Wilhelm." Ilse stood and strode from the room, leaving the rest of us in her wake.

After a minute or so, I broke the silence. "Right. Krystal, did that answer your question?"

"Yes, thank you."

"No problem. If you have any other questions, I did read the book once, so I might be able to help. I'm going to make it an early night. Bye." I left, ignoring the feeling that I was missing something important.

Chapter Thirteen

Information is Power

"I'm pretty sure that glaring at a textbook doesn't actually help you understand it any better," Phyna said, during one of our designated study times. It was a time when we could feel free to ignore each other to accomplish our own goals without either feeling rude. Which was why I was a little surprised she had noticed at all.

I tried to relax my features. She was right, and I was getting a headache. My third today. "Yeah, I know. I'm just having trouble keeping these interactions straight. Which is awful, because I know this one."

Phyna perched on the edge of the couch. "What seems to be the problem?"

"I'm trying to map out the chemical reaction of mixing ammonia and bleach. I know what it does, generally. It emits toxic fumes. But mapping out the entire process is a little harder."

"Toxic fumes?"

"Very toxic. Unfortunately, both bleach and ammonia are common cleaning ingredients so it's easy to do accidentally."

"Are they dangerous? When not mixed, I mean." Phyna looked at my paper.

I shrugged. "They aren't to be played with. I don't know about dragons, but humans are cautioned to use gloves if handling either of them. Last time I used bleach, I poured less than an ounce in a liter of water, didn't bother to use gloves, and ended up with all these micro cuts on my hands. Sure, they healed fine, but they were annoying, and I discovered them by eating popcorn." Phyna looked at me, uncomprehending. "Human food. Fluffy popped corn kernels, usually topped with butter and salt." Still nothing. "Salt really hurts when introduced to an open wound. Even a minor one."

"Oh, my sympathies." She looked to the ceiling. "I have seen corn, but it didn't look very fluffy."

"Right, it's a little different. You know, I have some microwave popcorn. Would you like to try some?"

Phyna twisted her head back to look at me, making me wonder about the spines of dragons. "If you do not mind sharing your food."

"Not at all. I need a break anyway." It only took a moment find a package in the cupboard. "I need to heat this up in the lounge. Be back in a few minutes."

Because we were on the first floor, we had the lobby on our floor, which took up a lot of space. But there was still a small lounge, a place we could meet for our floor meetings, and room to put things like microwaves and the washers/dryers.

I had finally asked Phyna why she was on the ground floor since flyers usually had room assignments on the higher floors, preferably with roof access. She said it was a matter of seniority. As a sophomore, she didn't have any. It was different in the freshman dorm.

No one was in the lounge, and the microwave was actually working. Sometimes technology was fritzy around here. Or, more accurately, sometimes in a school where a decent percent of the population had magic, elemental powers, and/or super human strength, some people were less than careful about where and how they used said powers. Higher quality technology was usually shielded against magic and physical damage, but the dorm microwaves weren't considered high priority.

When I went back to my room, fresh popcorn in hand, Phyna was reading over my chemistry homework. She peered up as I came in. "What is hydro–" she looked back at my notes, "clocic acid?"

"Hydrochloric?"

She re-read it. "Oops. Yes."

I offered her some popcorn. "Well, from the name, you can tell it's acidic, and it's made up of hydrogen and chlorine. It's a pretty strong acid, actually. I've seen it dissolve the shell off an egg in five minutes."

Phyna's head snapped up to look at me, popcorn forgotten. "A dragon egg?"

"What? No. Chicken egg. And it wasn't fertilized. Nothing would have hatched from it if it was left alone. I don't know how hard dragon eggs are compared to chicken eggs." Should have realized that Phyna probably thought differently about eggs than I did.

She nodded slowly. "I see."

"Um, it's also in the human stomach. That's how we dissolve food." Phyna eyed my midsection dubiously. "The stomach has a lining that allows it to handle the acid. But if we vomit, or some of the acid comes up as bile, which happens to everyone sometimes, it burns."

"Can it cause permanent damage?"

I had to think about it. "Maybe it could if you vomited a lot for a long time, but most people don't and the body naturally repairs itself. More uncomfortable than dangerous." Anyway, I didn't want to talk about that anymore. "Do you like the popcorn?"

Phyna delicately ate a kernel, then another. "It is a pleasant treat. The salt is what makes my mouth tingle?"

"Probably. Unless your taste buds are very different from mine. Both popcorn and butter by themselves are a little bland. Of course, this is microwave popcorn, so there are a few other chemicals thrown in. Mostly popcorn, butter, and salt, though." I offered her some more.

"Is popcorn a common treat among humans or a rare delicacy?"

I had to bite back a laugh. It was a fair question. "Well, popcorn, in and of itself, is a very common snack food. At least, in the country I'm from. In fact, when you ask an American to think of snack foods, popcorn will probably be in the top three to five choices. But there are also a lot of variations. Kettle corn has sugar and less salt.

Caramel corn has caramel. You can have cheese, or chocolate, or mix popcorn with other snack foods, even candy. Then there is gourmet popcorn. So, really it can be both."

She speared a kernel with a long claw. "A large prestige for a small food."

"You should look up regular corn some time. It's amazing. Some of the first settlers in my country would have died if the natives hadn't taught them how to grow corn. They introduced them to popcorn too."

"How can they be the first settlers if there were already natives? They were human natives, were they not?"

I winced. This was *not* something I wanted to go into. "Yes, they were humans. Okay, I'm not trying to justify this or anything. It happened long, long before I was born. But the people who came in from, mostly Europe, to settle in the United States largely pushed the natives aside to take the land. Yes, it was wrong. But it happened too long ago for anyone to do anything about. So, because most of the citizens living there now are descendants of settlers and immigrants, and I don't think the Native Americans kept written histories, we usually start history of the country from when the Europeans found it."

Phyna looked very confused. "This is considered right?"

"No, not really. Most people think it was wrong, but what do you do about something that happened centuries before you were born?"

Her tail was whipping around. "Do those natives consider taking their country back?"

"Not that I can tell. There aren't enough of them, for one. Two, I don't think most of them feel the need."

"Does your government oppress them to keep them in check?"

"No! Well, I suppose that depends on who you ask. I know they actually have certain privileges, like with taxes and stuff; but I also know that many of them live on reservations. They aren't required to, but many do." I sighed. "Honestly, it's not something I know a lot about. Most people just relegate it to past history, we can't do anything about it now, and ignore it. Kind of like an embarrassing secret. Only it isn't secret. Look, isn't there anything in dragon history that you really wish hadn't happened?"

Phyna ducked her head. "Yes, I think I see your point. But dragons live so long, 'history' is a little different."

"That makes sense." The United States was only a few centuries old. Ms. Grazletz had been the head librarian at Hyde for longer than my country had existed. Memories were probably stronger too. But I was done with this conversation, and Phyna seemed to be too. "Did you ever take Chemistry?"

"It was a little different. Mostly the effects of heat and cold on various objects and elements."

"Well, that is technically Chemistry. I think. Maybe chemistry and physics." I eyed my paper. Even to me, it looked like random gibberish. "So, what's your major?"

Phyna made a deep rumbling sound that I was pretty sure was the draconic equivalent to a sigh. "Tactical history."

"Huh, that's interesting." Also unexpected. "Do you like it?" Dumb question, Violet. If she didn't like it, she wouldn't be studying it.

"Not particularly."

Okay, maybe it wasn't a dumb question. "You don't? Then why…" She slumped. "Sorry. Look, it's none of my business. If you tell me to, I'll shut up and leave you alone about it."

There was no answer for a long time. I figured she didn't want to talk about it, so I crumpled up the now empty popcorn bag, tossed it in the direction of the trash, grimaced when I missed by a foot, huffed a silent laugh when Phyna hit the bag with her tail knocking it in the bin, and tried re-reading my text book. When she did start talking, I almost jumped.

"My family decided it would be advantageous for me to study it."

"Your family picked your major?" Wow, I was really glad I wasn't in that position. "Why that one?"

No one can grimace like a dragon. "That part I

would rather not discuss."

"Okay. Um, if it's not too much to ask, what would *you* have chosen to study?"

"Art," She answered immediately.

Also unexpected, but less so. Phyna had some absolutely gorgeous glass sculptures and vases and the like in the room that she said she had made. She mentioned doing mosaics too, but I hadn't seen any of them.

"You're good at art. I love your glass work. Does your family not consider art practical? I know that's sometimes the case for humans. Families sometimes disapprove of someone pursuing the arts because it is very hard to make a living in those fields."

"Aren't artists highly respected among humans? I was of the impression they were."

"Only the really, really, *really* good ones. For every famous artist, performer, writer, musician, etc. there are thousands more that never made it. For some reason, some people look down on them. Not sure why. I think it's partly cultural. America is a land of dreamers, but there is also a very practical bent in the majority. Dreams don't pay the bills, after all."

"They do if you're a dream interpreter." Phyna was completely serious.

"True. Also not a particularly respected career."

"It is among dragons."

"Which? Art or dream interpretation?"

"Both. But my family has other plans for me."

Should I say anything? Probably not. Was I going to say anything? Apparently so. "Look, like I said, it's none of my business, and heaven knows I am currently one of the last people qualified to give advice on family matters. But, it's *your* life. Are you really going to be happy if you spend your whole life doing what they want you to do? Of course, it's not easy being at odds with your family either. Right, I don't know anything. Ignore me."

She was laughing at me. She was trying to hide it, but the dragon was shaking enough to move the whole couch. "Did your family choose your major?"

"No. It was my choice to major in Biology. Mom suggested I look into being a doctor. I gave it some thought, took some first aid classes, but I couldn't walk that path. They never complained about it. Well, not much anyway. I know I didn't thrill anyone by breeding fruit flies to study genetics, or accidentally setting parts of the kitchen on fire with my chemistry set." The couch was now shaking hard enough that my vision was blurry. "But for the most part, they encouraged my interest in genetics. It's being at Hyde they are upset about. Though to be fair, they didn't even mind that in the beginning. I guess it's who I'm changing into that they mind." The couch stopped moving abruptly.

"Violet? Are you crying?"

"No." Water hit my shirt. "It's a leak. It's raining."

"There are five floors above us."

"Yeah, they should check into that." Another droplet fell. I could feel them on my face now. "I'm fine, really." My throat hurt. "I really am fine." I couldn't swallow anymore.

"Maybe… maybe you came home too early." I shrugged. "You've… declined, since returning. Maybe with Jesse having been hurt, you should be home. Maybe…"

"No, I can't. I'm fine. I just need… time." I had school, classes, and trying to figure out who was trying to close down the school. I couldn't leave now. And I couldn't let random emotions slow me down.

"Do you miss them? Your family?"

"Every single day."

***

My birthday passed quietly. I preferred it that way. It was about a week after the Pink Panther incident and three days after I broke down on Phyna, and I was definitely not up to a party. Honestly, part of me hoped my friends forgot. My birthday had gone horribly last year.

They didn't forget, but neither did anyone make a fuss of it. I got several birthday wishes, a few cards, a couple of small gifts, and we all ate dinner together. Mom called me, and I was able to talk to everyone, including Uncle Jack, Aunt Laura, and my cousins. Jesse was doing a lot better, but still had a ways to go until he counted as fully recovered. He promised to update me every week. I told him that he'd better. Like last year, they had sent a package, but it hadn't gotten to me yet. I promised to let them know when I got it.

It was nice to hear from them. It would have been even nicer if it didn't make me so homesick that I literally slid to the floor, legs unable to support me. I had recovered by the time Phyna came back, so I didn't tell her what happened. Or that it was my birthday. When I finally went to bed, all I could think about was that somehow my birthday managed to be even more depressing this year than it had last year.

***

The next day, Ilse snagged me as I was heading to my dorm. Literally. I was just walking when she came up behind me, grabbed my arm and started steering me in a different direction. "Ilse?" I tried pulling away. We had too much trouble with imposters for me to be comfortable with any of my friends acting strangely. Not to mention, it was seriously early for Ilse to be up.

She didn't say a word, but she did take her free hand and wrap it around her other hand like a bracelet. One of our codes. *Trust me. Don't talk.* Okay, then. Yeah, this wasn't creepy at all.

We went to the Barker Central building, and headed down. Past the first underground level that was well-lit, walled, and basically another floor. Past the second level, that was lit, but mostly dirt and rock. Into the third level that was rock hewn with no external lighting.

I couldn't see what she did, but Ilse soon had a glowing red stone in her hand. They were used like flashlights by some of the people at the school, particularly those sensitive to bright lights or certain parts of the light spectrum. The campus bookstore sold them.

Right, I could do this. Adrian had actually given me a Taser like he teased, and I carried it on me, like he made me promise. If this was a trap, I wasn't completely helpless.

Ilse let go of my arm and handed me a second, unlit stone. When I didn't do anything, she took the stone again, tapped it against the wall twice, and put the now lit stone back in my hand. So I had a Taser and a rock if this was a trap. And my arm was free, which made maneuvering a little easier.

We walked about twenty yards when we turned a corner and spotted two other people standing ten or so yards away, also with glow-y stones. As we moved closer, I saw that it was Adrian and Kara. Okay, not a trap. Or if it was, it was bigger than anything I had run into yet.

Not a word was spoken. Adrian took point, leading us through the most tangled, convoluted path I had ever seen, before ending up in a cavern of a room. The rest of the group was there, most sitting on the ground with a glowing stone nearby. Ilse signed something to Adrian that wasn't part of our code. He nodded. She took something small out of her pocket and placed it at the door.

"No one can hear us here." Ilse declared. She sat on the ground, looking more graceful doing so than I thought was possible, before tapping her stone to the ground. It got brighter. I did the same, noticing that some people had already brightened theirs.

"Is that a government level privacy ward?" Tim asked.

"Yes. Wilhelm had to make some complex arrangements to get it to me."

"Don't they only work if there's nothing already planted?" Krystal asked.

"Yes and no. It will cancel any eavesdropping spells on a person, but not ones planted on a room. Which is why I checked this room for magic." Adrian waved a small device that looked a little like a cell phone to me. "Don't even ask how I got this. Anyway, the only things here are the normal wards. Fire protection, air refreshing, anti-damage. This," he pulled out another device, "scrambles electronics within fifty feet."

"Okay, not to naysay, but is this level of paranoia quite necessary?" I asked. Most of the group looked as puzzled as I did. So I wasn't the only one who missed the memo.

"Yes." Ilse said. "When we were in the library, you mentioned about video cameras and listening devices."

"True, but I don't think most people here at Hyde would bother with that."

"While there, I mentioned the need to contact my brother." There were a few nods. "I went directly to my room, wrote a message, and sent it. The entire process took under thirty minutes."

Still not seeing the point.

"That message was intercepted and read."

Oh, that was the point. "What? Are you sure?" I asked. Along with a few others.

"I am certain. The message was a silly little code that we invented some time ago that basically meant 'I am testing this delivery method.' Wilhelm tested the message and found evidence of tampering. He sent me back a message, also in code, telling me so, and had the privacy ward delivered to me by private courier. My letter had also been tampered with."

"Why would someone intercept your mail?" Kara asked.

"There are three possibilities I can see. One, someone is watching either Wilhelm or me personally, likely because of our positions within the council. In which case, the rest of you are unlikely to be affected. Two, our mail is checked regularly, either as something the school does to students, or to us in particular, because of our tendency to become involved in 'interesting' situations." Ilse looked around. "Or, because someone was listening to us that day in the library. Perhaps was always listening."

"O…kay. Those are some scary thoughts." My breathing was shaky. "What on earth did we say in the library?"

"What if it wasn't just the library?" Denise asked, as serious as I've ever seen her. "Do you know how many conversations I've managed to hear by staying still and listening as a dragonfly? I promise I'm not the only one."

"Who is high enough to intercept mail?" Krystal asked.

"What if there is something on one of us? A listening device or spell," Tim asked.

All these were said about the same time. And they were all good questions. But we couldn't solve anything if we were freaking out and talking over each other, which was getting worse as everyone got more agitated. I clapped twice. Everyone stopped talking.

"Right, priorities. First, Tim. I think that's a good point. We should figure out if any of us is carrying a listening device or spell. Then we can work on figuring out who could have intercepted mail, what might have been said where, and where we can talk without anyone listening."

"We can talk here." Adrian waved a hand around. "This is under the cafeteria. Any locator spells will be confused by the presence of so many other students. They aren't good at exact location or depth. Any listening spells of us would be cancelled out by the ward, just like electronics are stopped by the scrambler. I'll give us all a scan before we leave."

"How do you know about this place?" Kara asked.

"Several months of being an outcast and having a lot of free time. I've mapped out the entire school underground. My maps are more accurate than the ones in the library. Speaking of which, I made a copy for everyone, using a copier that *isn't* located on this island." He spoke the first part fast, and the second part forcefully. Not something he wanted to talk about, obviously.

I had a copy of Adrian's map, but I really hadn't used it much. The upper tunnel level was pretty well marked and that's what I used most of the time. Still, I took my copy with the others, and noticed that some particular rooms were marked as possible meeting places.

While there was no way to know for sure if it only that one time, or just in the library, or if someone had been listening to us every time we met, we did try to figure out what we had said when and where. Easier said than done.

"They don't know our code. Or at least, I was able to tell that the 'Ilse' next to me was an imposter, because she didn't know either of our codes," I said. "We decided on those while we met under Price."

"I do not believe that we ever actually mentioned

that we had sworn an oath or the implications of said oath while meeting in the library," Tim said. "I may have been mistaken about that, however."

"Even if we didn't mention the oath itself, we did a lot of research in the library. If someone listening to us could access the list of what books we checked out…" Allison trailed off.

This was going to be a bigger problem than we thought. It was so hard to figure out what we discussed where, and we still didn't know if this was a random fluke or not.

"How were you able to tell someone read your mail?" Bria asked.

"I have a seal I can place on the envelope as I close it. Not a wax seal, though I do have one of those as well. However, if someone opens the envelope without touching the matching seal to it first, an hour after being opened, the paper turns red if held to a candle."

"Meaning, they could have been reading all our mail, the whole time?" I asked. "After all, I don't think the rest of us have ways to check like that." Actually, I hadn't written actual, physical letters to my family. I had sent emails and phone calls. Would that actually be safer, or were those even easier to intercept? How deep did this go?

"I have sent messages to Wilhelm and my parents previously. Nothing was said about any failure in security. Still, it could have been a random check, with the return letter checked solely because the first letter was so unusual."

"Does everyone have a post office or equivalent on the mainland of their home dimension?" I asked. We all did. "Well, we can use that for mail. But meeting spots are going to be harder. Especially if we don't dare use the library anymore."

"Which is why I labeled the six best meeting spots in the underground," Adrian sounded a pinch smug. "If we use them randomly, coming at separate times, no one should catch on. Denise or I can scout ahead. If she's a dragonfly, most won't even see her; and people are used to me being down here. I've been here often enough. Seriously, you could live here if you had to." I looked at the places labeled one through six, spread between the three underground levels.

"But do we always have to meet underground?" Allison asked. "Aren't there ways to safeguard conversations above ground too?" She never did like meeting underground, probably the bird in her. "Sure you need walls for a privacy ward to latch on to, but there are rooms where students can meet. It should be the same process as checking underground."

"Little easier to be spotted, but if we keep changing things up, we should be okay," Bria agreed.

"We also have to make sure we don't always disappear for long periods of time, because that looks suspicious," I pointed out. We had been here nearly an hour, and I didn't know about anyone else, but my legs were cramping up.

There was a general agreement. "Fine. I'll scan everyone, and we'll all scout out a few more places where we can meet and try to figure out who might have opportunity and interest in reading people's mail." Adrian stood up.

Ilse stood next. "Suppose we meet at meeting place four in twenty-four hours to compare notes."

We agreed. Adrian ran his magic scanner over himself, head to shoes. There were a few colors by his head and heart, same colors. They seemed to mostly match the colors I had seen when Linda Green did a magic reading on me. His coat glowed brightly. He looked over the results. "Looks like the normal spells. A listening spell would have to latch onto an object. The coat's already enchanted, it resists any other spells. Nothing else of mine glowed."

He did Allison next. Her earing glowed. "Anti-theft charms." While I might not have been the only one here from a shade dimension, I was the only one who hadn't known about the dimensions before I got here. It made sense that most of my friends had some magical objects. I could have acquired a few myself, but they tended to be more expensive than I wanted to consider.

One by one, Adrian checked us all. Everything that lit up had an explanation, and the owner was aware of the spell. When he came up to me, I wasn't expecting anything but the spells Linda had told me about. So I was as shocked as everyone else when my amber bracelet lit up like Times Square.

Chapter Fourteen

Betrayed?

"Phyna said it was a good luck charm." I stared at the bracelet. "She didn't say anything about it being magical."

"Most lucky charms are not." Ilse peered at the scanner. I'm sure she didn't mean for that to be funny.

"I can't tell what this is. It's complex, very complex. More than this scanner was meant to handle. No listening spells. But I think," Adrian scowled. "I'm taking you to the infirmary. Now. They can figure out what this is. Don't take it off!" I froze. "I'm seeing a partially integrated spell. Removing the bracelet could cause a nasty backlash. Have you taken it off since Phyna gave it to you?"

"No, she said not to." And I had never questioned it. Not once.

"Maybe a small compulsion. To leave it in place." Adrian tossed Ilse his scanner. "Can you finish up here?"

"I can." Ilse nodded regally.

"Shouldn't we report this?" Tim asked.

"First get to the infirmary and get this dealt with. Then we can know *what* to report," Adrian said.

"Besides, maybe Phyna acted in good faith, or the

spell was put on later. Or maybe it is really a very complicated good luck charm. No point in acting accusatory before we have more information," I said. I really didn't want to believe Phyna would want to hurt me. And if it turned out we were wrong and the spell was harmless, I didn't want to hurt her feelings either.

"Good plan. Now, *let's go!*" Adrian escorted me out at a brisk pace.

We had to go up a couple levels, but the infirmary wasn't far from the cafeteria, so we made good time. Reaching the infirmary, I was suddenly struck by just how dumb this whole thing sounded. Seriously, what was I supposed to say? 'Hi, I think my roommate may have given me a cursed bracelet. Could you check it for me?' When the receptionist, a six-armed naga, asked why we were here, I couldn't even answer.

"Hello, my friend here hasn't been feeling well lately," Adrian said smoothly. "Worn out, run down, moody."

"Adrian!"

"Snappish." He dodged my elbow. "Honestly, we're concerned. All of us."

Quite frankly, I had gotten concerned myself. While I had resisted coming to the infirmary, maybe getting the bracelet looked at under the guise of being checked over wasn't a bad idea. "I have been exhibiting some symptoms of depression," I confessed.

Adrian raised an eyebrow. "You admitted it? I

thought we might have to drag you here and bribe a doctor to examine you."

I huffed in mild annoyance.

"You have the choice between Dr. Zyloas, Dr. Arken, and Nurse Persephone," The receptionist said, looking at her computer screens. She had two, right next to each other.

I had no idea who Dr. Arken was. Dr. Zyloas was a zombie. I'm sure she was a nice person, very intelligent, but even with having Dr. Rigor, another zombie, for a professor, I was still having trouble with the 'zombie' part. Plus, zombies can't see or undo magic. Nurse Persephone, I had seen a few times, and she could see and undo magic. "Nurse Persephone, please."

"Very well, if you would take a seat, you will be called back when she is ready for you." The naga woman turned to Adrian. "You will not be permitted back with your friend, but you may wait in the waiting room."

He nodded, and we both took seats in the color monstrosity they called a waiting room. I have no idea who decided that neon orange should be paired with radioactive green and fluorescent pink, but I hope they got fired. We couldn't talk about why we were really here, and Adrian isn't a big talker anyway. I couldn't think of a thing to say. Waiting rooms make me nervous in the best of times, and the times I was in waiting rooms were rarely the best of times. This didn't even come close.

I fidget when I'm nervous. But it wasn't until

Adrian's hand came out and caught mine, making me jump, that I realized I was fiddling with the amber bracelet. Yeah, probably better not to touch that any more than I had to.

"Do that a lot?"

"Probably. I fiddle with things a lot. Broke at least two watchbands that way. And I've been stressed lately." I rubbed at my eyes. "Is there a water fountain? I really need some water." I felt vaguely like I might throw up. Sometimes that was a sign of dehydration for me. Besides, my mouth was dry.

"No, but there is a water cooler. I'll get some. You look… less than good."

Considering how I felt, that was a compliment. He was back with cold water a minute later. I drank half in my first swallow, then held the cup to my forehead, closing my eyes.

"You okay?"

"I don't like this place. It's an abomination to the eyes, and I have terrible memories of this place."

I opened my eyes in time to see Adrian's eyes dart to the bracelet. I shrugged. Possible. Would make sense that if there was a spell that wasn't supposed to be there, then there might be some aversion techniques to keep me away from places where that spell might be noticed.

"Do you know why they chose this color cacophony?" Not that I expected him to know, but it was something I was mildly curious about. And it had nothing to do with my possibly wearing cursed jewelry.

"You didn't know? These are the most common warning colors among the different races. Ever species that attends Hyde uses one or more of these colors to signify warnings or danger. There's also a few in the infrared and ultraviolet that you can't see, but are perceiving anyway. It makes everything seem even more overwhelming and bright."

"Really?" I squinted. "That *is* hazard cone orange, isn't it?"

"Sure is. They are also extremely visible due to their placement in the color spectrum."

"Can't argue that. But why put hazard colors in the infirmary?"

"So you know where to go to resolve your problems."

Nurse Persephone came out before I could say anything else. "Violet Peters? Oh, you. I don't think you've ever come here for a not immediate need."

I followed her into the examination room. "No offence to you or any other dedicated health care professional, but I don't like hospitals."

"Hm," She smiled, blue face beaming. "Most do not. And if you are suffering from depression, it's not surprising you had neither the energy nor the inclination to seek help. When did your symptoms begin?"

"Well, there was a family emergency, back in late August. My cousin nearly died. I went home. He recovered, but…" I bit my lip. "Actually, I felt terrible when I came back here, and I don't think I've felt quite well since."

The nurse frowned. "Define 'terrible'."

"Okay, at the airport," I paused, but she seemed to either understand or not care what an airport was, "I felt shaky and nauseous. At first, I thought it was nerves, stress, or maybe homesickness kicking in early. Then I actually passed out on takeoff. Things haven't been as bad since, but I have headaches, I'm homesick a lot. No energy. A few days ago, I joined some friends to watch cartoons. They all laughed at the funny parts. I didn't."

"Hmm. Anything else?"

"I can't concentrate on schoolwork. I'm having trouble with work I know I can do."

Yup, she was concerned. "You should have come in earlier. There isn't a scan for depression per se, but I would like to check you over for some possible side effects and other possible causes."

I nodded. Nurse Persephone's eyes glowed white, magenta hair flying, as she looked me over, stopping at my wrist. "Hold out your arm." I did so. "I need to consult with my colleague for a minute. Please don't move, and don't touch anything."

"O…kay." Well, mission somewhat accomplished.

She left, coming back a few minutes later with a human looking man. About six foot, brown hair and eyes, skinny as a pencil. "Hi, Violet. I'm Dr. Arken. I hear you may be having some problems with depression."

"Depression, and maybe my arm or bracelet."

He smiled thinly. "So I hear. May I take a look?"

I moved my still held out arm so it was more in front of him. Dr. Arken put on some glasses that even I could tell were enchanted. The longer he looked, the deeper he frowned. "Wow. Honestly, I'm surprised you're still standing."

"That… sounds really bad." What had Phyna done to me?"

"There is a partially integrated compulsion spell on this. If it had fully integrated, you would either have done, or be doing whatever the compulsion is, but you'd be fine. Probably. It depends on what the compulsion was. If you had resisted it entirely, you'd be fine. But it's partially taken hold, and you're resisting. Something else, that previously took root, is fighting the compulsion, and you're suffering the consequences, both of the compulsion, and the fighting. Possibly whatever is fighting it as well." He looked up at me sharply. "Where did you get this?"

"Someone gave it to me. She said it was good luck.

"Yeah, well, either she was wrong, she lied, or someone enspelled it after you put it on." He straightened. "I'm guessing you do not wish to have this unknown compulsion on you? As I thought. We have a few options available. We can take all the spells off and remove the bracelet. You'll be completely fine, but we won't be able to track down who did this or what they wanted. Option two, we can dampen some of the spells in the bracelet to take it off, but that would complicate finding who did it, and probably, what they wanted. Option three, we put a temporary magic nullifier on you, hope you don't pass out or have a heart attack from the sudden stop of the compulsion and whatever is fighting it, and take off the bracelet then. The third is the riskiest to your health, but the easiest to analyze the magic."

"How risky are the first two options?"

Dr. Arken sighed. "I'm not going to lie. They all have some risk. We *don't know* what the bracelet is spelled to do. Or what tripwires it may have. Because of that, there is the chance of missing one. Or it may be harmless. Assuming that we don't miss a lethal tripwire, removing the spells completely has little chance of harming you. Dampening them is a little higher, but still less than a ten percent chance of causing serious risk."

"Lethal tripwire? Is that likely?" Why had I ever put this stupid bracelet on in the first place?

"Probably not. But we can't tell. Even if there was a lethal tripwire, nullifying the magic entirely, it wouldn't go off. However, this has already shown to have strong effects on your health. The risk of a heart attack is very low, and we should be able to deal with it quickly if something did happen, but it is a chance."

"What would happen if I just took off the bracelet?" I asked.

"We don't know. We don't know what's on it, and what kind of failsafes it has. Maybe nothing will happen. Maybe it will try to kill you if unclasped. Or your arm might explode. That's why we need to remove or dampen the magic first."

I swallowed hard. This was so very not what I had been expecting when I woke up this morning. "Why can't you tell what's on it?"

"It takes time and supplies to study a complex enchanted item. Sometime it takes even more to track down the castor." Dr. Arken gave me a steady but sympathetic look. "The choice is completely yours. I would say you can have as long as you like to decide, but you are going to continue to suffer until this is dealt with."

Biting my lips, I closed my eyes and tried to think. We *needed* to know who did this and why. But did I really have to risk my life to find out? A shaky laugh burst from me, startling the two health professionals. I had been risking my life since I got here. Why should now be any different? "Sorry. Just… Sorry. Unless you think it has more than a twenty percent or so chance of killing me or causing permanent damage, I want to go with the nullifier. I need to know who cast this and what they cast."

Dr. Arken nodded. "I'd put your chances of serious risk to be more in the ten to fifteen percent range. One more time, the nullifier is your choice?"

Deep breath in. Deep breath out. "Yes. I choose the nullifier."

"I would probably do the same. It will take a few minutes to gather supplies. Stay here, and don't touch the bracelet."

They came back with a large black stone the size of my fist, and three silver metal stars that were a little smaller. "I should warn you," Nurse Persephone said, as she motioned for me to lie down. "We do not know what is currently fighting your compulsion, and it doesn't look like the result of a spell. There is a small chance that it will not be completely stopped with this process, though it will be very weakened. Once the compulsion is removed, you should be able to tell what the compulsion was intended to make you do. From there we can ascertain what was fighting it."

I nodded. Then stopped as a metal star was placed on my forehead.

"Before we begin," Dr. Arken lifted my hand, positioning the stone so my bracelet rested on top of it, while Nurse Persephone put a second star on my heart. "Can you tell me who gave you this bracelet? There will be a complete investigation if you wish, but it's a place to start."

Should I say? I still didn't know if it was her fault. But I didn't know it wasn't either. "It was…" Nothing came out. Why not? I told my friends it was Phyna, back when she gave it to me. But I couldn't tell these doctors?"

They looked at each other and nodded. "Don't

worry about it. You can tell us after." Dr. Arken put the third star over the top of the bracelet, then pulled out a fourth star in gold that he held. "This will probably be very unpleasant. It may even be painful. Nurse Persephone will be keeping an eye out for physical stress to your organs. Stopping midway is even riskier than completing, so please try to keep still. No matter what, it shouldn't take more than a few minutes. Last chance to choose a different option."

"No." I took a deep breath. "I'm ready." My eyes snapped shut and I waited.

Apparently, no, I was not ready. Something was leeching out of my very bones and sinews, clawing, trying to stay. I couldn't have opened my eyes if I wanted to, and I don't think I would have been able to see if I did. Lightning was in my bloodstream, burning me from the inside out. My spirit, my essence, my inner core was being tampered with. Then there was nothing. Absolutely nothing. I didn't even exist.

A small click exploded in my ear drums. I was a feather, floating in the wind, gently landing in my own body, as they removed the stone and stars. "How do you feel?"

My eyes blinked open. I wasn't in pain, wasn't sad. I was practically giddy, actually. "Wonderful. Wow, it's like being weightless." I giggled. "I had forgotten it was possible to feel like this."

"Do you feel a lack of desire to do something? Something you felt driven to do before?" Nurse Persephone added to her previous question.

I sat up, after checking that I could. "No… No, I don– Oh!" I wasn't homesick. "Oh, wow. I don't want to go home now." The oath must have been what was fighting the compulsion. Previously 'installed', taken voluntarily, and probably deeply rooted. No wonder I felt terrible.

They exchanged another glance. "Who gave you this?" Dr. Arken asked.

"Her name's Phyna. She's my roommate. But I don't understand. She's never had a problem with me before." That I knew of. Then again, it wouldn't be the first time I turned out to misread someone completely.

"It's possible that she was unaware of the nature of the bracelet, that the spell was put on after she gave it to you, or that she was under a compulsion herself." Nurse Persephone and Dr. Arken worked in concert to carefully put the bracelet in a wooden box without either of them directly touching it themselves. "We will investigate. I do not recommend confronting her."

No, I had no desire to confront a dragon that might wish me harm while acting like my friend. But I would try to give her the benefit of the doubt for now.

"It will probably take at least a month before we can fully analyze these spells, but I *can* give you something that will prevent new spells from taking hold of you. It won't affect any current spells." Dr. Arken removed his gloves.

"I would like that."

He came back with a pill bottle. "One a day. It will take at least twenty minutes to take full effectiveness, and each lasts twenty-four hours. Either avoid people during that time, or try to take the pill as the last one is wearing off. I can get you a watch charmed to remind you."

"Thank you." I read the bottle. Take one daily with water, preferably not on an empty stomach, do not overlap by more than an hour. Potential side effects for races who are not magical seemed limited to mild nausea, and occasional hindrances with the translation spell. Right, I could do that.

"I've given you a forty day supply. They aren't addictive, if for some reason you want a refill, but still not something you want to be taking long term." He handed me a watch. Utilitarian looking, white face, black numbers, black band. I put it on and took the first pill. As I swallowed, the watch lit up, and a golden hand appeared, did a sweep of the face, ending at the twelve. "Because this is a once a day pill, the golden hand will move every two hours. Very common for medicine reminders. If you are concerned about your roommate, do not go straight home. We will be reporting this to security for you. Your RA and RD will probably want to speak to you shortly."

"I understand."

They let me leave then. Adrian was still waiting, idly flipping through one of the magazines in the waiting room. It appeared to be about pottery. He looked up as I came out. "How are you feeling?"

"Amazing."

He quirked an eyebrow at me. "Uh, good?"

"Yes. I don't feel sick, or sad, or homesick."

"Good." He looked towards my wrist. "They were able to take it off okay?"

"Yeah, and my arm didn't even explode or anything!" Okay, maybe I was a little too giddy.

Adrian looked like he wasn't sure if he should be concerned or amused. "Well, I'm glad about that. What was on it?"

"They're going to test it to see exactly what was on it and who cast it. But I'm not feeling depressed and desperate to go home anymore." We left and I quietly explained what they had said. They had forgotten to investigate what might be fighting the spell. Since I didn't want to explain the oath, I wasn't going to remind them.

"So, what are you going to do about Phyna?"

That cut some of my giddy elation. "I don't know. I don't want to believe that she'd want to hurt me, I've known her almost as long as I've known Ilse. True, it looks like it was mostly a compulsion to go home. Still…"

"Still, you haven't seen a reason not to trust her before now. Has she urged you to go home?"

I sighed. "Yeah, actually. After Jesse…, well, she kept suggesting I should be home with my family."

"Family is very important for dragons. It's completely possible that she would suggest that anyway. What did you tell her anyway?"

"Not much." I tried one of the memory techniques Ilse had taught me. "I didn't want to talk about it, so I just said my cou…" I missed the next step. Adrian caught me before I kissed the sidewalk.

"Violet?"

"I said *my cousin* was in the hospital and might not make it. When I came back, she asked me, 'How's *Jesse*?'. I didn't name him. Never said what was wrong, but she knew he had been hurt, not sick."

"You sure you never mentioned his name?"

"As sure as I can be." And I had missed this completely.

"Right, did she meet him while he was here?"

I shrugged. "I never introduced them, neither of them mentioned meeting the other."

"Okay, so they might have met. But she's a dragon. They have lots of relatives. She shouldn't have assumed you had just one cousin, especially since you don't. It isn't proof of anything."

"No, but it is suspicious."

"Right. Be very careful." We were at my dorm now. "Maybe you shouldn't go in."

It would have been a lie to say I wasn't nervous, but what was I supposed to do? Phyna had never done anything to me directly. Security would talk to her, probably soon. I needed to be where they could find me. "I have to at some point. If I'm not up to my ears in this mess, I'll see you for dinner tonight. Nine o'clock? Ilse will probably be there too. That way we can fill in some others."

Adrian shuffled his weight. "I don't like it. You have your Taser?"

"Yes."

"That's something."

"If you think I'd succeed in taking on a dragon with a Taser, you're crazy." He smiled a little. "It'll be fine. She can't do anything to me directly. Probably as soon as the investigation officially starts, one or both of us will be assigned different rooms."

"Maybe you should pack an emergency bag. Make things faster if they do."

Not a bad idea. "I might at that. Now, I need to go. See you tonight." I gave Adrian a quick kiss and headed in.

The closer I got to my room, the more nervous I got. So, I stalled. Before I went to class, I had started some laundry in the washer. Originally, I would have only been gone about an hour. It was definitely done, so I tossed it in the dryer. What else could I do out here?

Finally I couldn't stall anymore and went back to my room. Phyna was there, on the computer. "Oh, hi. You've been out awhile." Was she looking at my wrist? Did she notice?

I shrugged. "Things to do. How are you doing?"

"Fine. You? You seem… lighter."

"I feel lighter. I feel better than I have in a while."

Her tail twitched and wrapped around the leg of the desk. "Good. I'm glad. Oh, did you need the computer?"

"Not right now. Maybe later." I had no idea what to do. There was a reason I never went into acting. "Hey, Phyna? Did you meet Jesse while he was here?"

"No. Why?"

"Oh, I was just curious. Um, if you'll excuse me, I have some things to do." I disappeared into my room almost before she could say she didn't mind.

Adrian had a good idea about packing a quick bag. I had a spare backpack that would work perfectly. Two or three changes of clothes, toiletries, my journal, bears, my jewelry, etc. Basically the small stuff that I didn't want anyone else going through. It didn't take long to pack, and I stuck the bag in the closet. Not as obvious there.

I tried very hard to read my botany text book, but my concentration was lousy. At least this time it was from nervousness, not a spell. Unfortunately, botany was my weakest point of biology. There was just something about trying to memorize the parts of plants that was mind-numbingly boring. I was trying though. It was almost a relief when it was time to fetch my laundry.

Phyna was still at the computer desk. "Going out again?"

"Laundry. Be back in a few minutes."

"Is that bleach?" Her tail point towards the white container I had dropped near the door when I came in from starting the wash.

"Yes. Sorry, I should have put that away. I'll get it when I come back."

"No hurry."

I went to the lounge/laundry room, taking my collapsible basket with me. The doors closed automatically behind me, and I took a few minutes to fold the clothes. They weren't *neatly* folded, but I tried not to be a complete slob. Sometimes, anyway.

Clothes folded, I reached for the door knob. It didn't turn. I jiggled the knob. Nothing. The door was stuck. It did that sometimes. I put the basket down and tried to get a good grip on the handle. It jerked, but didn't open. I tried the other way. Nothing.

Leaning on the door, I grabbed the handle with

both hands and turned as hard as I could. Almost had it, a little more. When I thought I had the knob turned, I pushed hard at the door. It moved about half an inch. I pushed harder and it reluctantly opened enough that I could get out. Shaking my head, I grabbed my laundry, making a note to mention the door to the RA. They needed to fix that.

When I was about halfway to my room, the door started to glow blue, and an alarm went off. The alarm that said someone was badly hurt.

I dropped the basket and ran, digging the keys out of my pocked as I did. Haste made me clumsy, and it took two tries to unlock the door. Vaguely, I could see and hear other people popping out of their rooms to see what was going on.

Throwing the door open, I suddenly couldn't breathe. The very air burned. Tears blurred my eyes, as I rapidly turned a handkerchief into an emergency air mask. What happened?

There! On the table was a bucket. By the bucket was my bleach container and one of my cleaning sprays. My eyes were watering too much to read it, but the spray must have had ammonia. "Phyna? Where are you?" I shouted. Or tried to.

First, I had to get rid of the bucket. We only had one window, but at least we had that. I dashed to the window and forced it open. Then I grabbed the bucket and dumped it outside. It would kill the grass, but the fumes should dissipate quickly.

Someone was behind me. Someone with hooves. Clindoque? "What happened?" Clindoque asked, then started choking.

I gave a hunched shrug that I'm not sure she saw, trying to wave air out the window while looking for Phyna. She was slumped on the floor near the computer desk.

I fell to my knees next to her and tried to check if she was breathing. I had no idea how this would affect her, or even what she thought she was doing. The only way to tell she was breathing was to hold a hand in front of her nostrils. She was. "Help me get her out of here!"

With the help of Clindoque and Tryta, a troll from a few doors down, we got Phyna out into the hallway. I closed the door so the fumes wouldn't affect anyone else. Hopefully the window would air the room out enough.

"What happened?" Clindoque asked again.

"I have no idea! I just went to get my laundry. Everything was fine when I left. I don't know why she would do that."

"Do what?" Clindoque held up a hand, then looked around. "Okay, show's over! Did someone call the infirmary?" Before anyone answered, a healer was teleported in. "Good. If you don't need to be here, time to leave. Violet, stay here."

The healer, one of the furry flippered people, whose race name I was always forgetting, started examining Phyna. "Can you tell me what happened?"

"She mixed bleach and ammonia. Combined, they make toxic fumes. I don't know *why* she would do that, because we talked about it a few days ago. About how dangerous it was. I was getting my laundry, and came back to find…" I trailed off and took a shaky breath. Was this a suicide attempt? Had she realized that I knew she had been up to something, and done this deliberately so she wouldn't have to face the consequences? I wiped away a tear. "Will she be okay?"

"She'll recover." The healer was holding a flipper over her neck. They had the ability to heal with a touch, but I wasn't sure if that worked if they couldn't see the injury.

Phyna coughed and opened her eyes. She saw me and started to whisper in a hoarse voice. "Violet, why?"

Wait, what?

***

We were separated while the whole event was investigated. Separated and kept isolated. Well, I was. They put me in a room in Barker. Phyna was taken to the infirmary for observation. They said something about keeping her overnight. Considering there was a bed in this room, I was probably also being kept overnight.

Taria showed up after I had paced the mostly blank room for about an hour. "I need your side of the story."

"Okay, it's a long story."

"Start with the ammonia and bleach." I quickly explained the conversation we had a few days ago. "And today?'

"Today I did laundry. I left the bleach container in the sitting room. Phyna pointed it out, and I apologized and said I'd put it away when I came back from getting my wash from the dryer. I was heading back when the door went blue."

"Did you touch the bleach today?"

"Yes, I poured some in my laundry."

"How about the ammonia?"

"I don't think so. I don't remember."

"Did you mix these chemicals?"

"No! Absolutely not."

Taria leaned back, expressionless. "Did anything odd happen between you and Phyna recently?"

I sighed. "This wasn't how I wanted it to come out, but Phyna gave me a bracelet, just before I left for home. Today I went to the infirmary, for signs of depression, and they found a compulsion on it. It had partially integrated. They had to use a magic nullifier to remove it, so they could study it, find out what it was for. All I know is that I didn't feel depressed and homesick afterwards."

Taria's wings flared out, filling the room. "Who

did? Who did you see?"

"Nurse Persephone and… um, Doctor… Arken! That was his name."

"Did you confront Phyna about this?"

"No. I wanted to let security handle things. The infirmary said it would take time to analyze the bracelet and find out who actually cast the spell. So, I didn't say a word."

Taria was silent for a long few minutes. "Phyna says you mixed the chemicals before you left and said it was important that she not touch it."

"No, I never did!"

"I read her mind." I started to relax. "She isn't lying."

Chapter Fifteen

From Bad to Worse

"But, that's impossible! Or, maybe... Look, I didn't do anything!"

"Yet, there is no way to prove that. All the evidence says you did." Taria looked at me steadily.

"I would never do something like that."

"You have been acting odd for some time. Secretive, isolated, closed off." I couldn't really argue with that. The last few weeks I hadn't wanted to spend time with other people. "My oath requires me to treat all students equally. If you are found guilty, at minimum, you will be expelled. At maximum, you could be charged with Interdimensional criminal charges. Ms. Grazletz is heavily pushing that option."

This was a nightmare. That was all. It couldn't be real. "How can I prove I'm innocent?"

"I do not know. I cannot read your mind. I can read Phyna's, which says you are guilty. Your fingerprints are on both the bleach and ammonia. There is no magic involved. It is simply your word against hers. And right now, it looks like she's telling the truth."

"What about a truth spell on me?" I had read about those.

Somehow, Taria's face got even more

expressionless. "No spell can be cast on you for at least twenty hours, thanks to your pill from the infirmary. It is possible that your status as a closed mind would interfere with the spells accuracy in the first place, and many are capable of finding ways around a truth spell if given enough time to prepare. No, a truth spell on you would not be considered sufficient, even if you did proclaim your innocence under one."

Groaning, I buried my head in my hands, pulling at my hair. "I think Phyna was trying to make me leave Hyde. That's what the compulsion seemed to be."

"Is that why you attacked her this way? Because she *might* have done something to you?" Like a punch to the gut, I suddenly realized that even Taria didn't believe me.

"I didn't attack her! This is a smokescreen. A distraction."

Her wings folded into scrolls. "Tomorrow, there will be a trial. Phyna's mind will be read again. Unless you can find a way to prove your innocence there, you *will* be found guilty. I cannot treat you differently than any other student. Consider that, and what you know of Interdimensional Law. A meal will be brought to you in two hours, and another at eight in the morning. There is a bathroom at the end of the hall, to the left. Attempting to leave the corridor will set off an alarm. Goodnight."

As soon as she left, I threw myself backwards onto the plain cot, searching the ceiling as if it had the answers. I certainly didn't. The bracelet couldn't be analyzed by tomorrow, and there was no guarantee that

Phyna had cast whatever spells were on it anyway. She probably hadn't. Even if she had, that didn't prove I hadn't set her up with the chemicals.

How had she fooled Taria? I knew it was possible to block a telepath from your head, but to show fake memories? Or maybe someone planted those memories for her. Right now, it was possible that Phyna believed what she said.

There was no time. How could I prove *anything* by tomorrow? Especially if I couldn't leave here. For the first time, I really wished I wasn't a closed mind.

Taria didn't believe I was innocent. Even if she did, she would have to judge based on the evidence, which was pretty flagrantly against me. But expelling me would mean the school was without a human, something she desperately wanted to avoid. I had checked, there were no new humans this semester. Even as upset as I was, I could dredge up some sympathy for the purple immortal.

So, if *I* was stuck in that catch-22, what would I do? She had a plan, or an idea, at least. I got a distinct feel of a subtle message being passed on. Okay, she thinks I'm guilty, or at least, could be guilty. She has to expel me. But she can't. What did she say that she didn't have to say?

She told me to consider what I knew of Interdimensional Law, which wasn't much. I knew it could be strict, probably because there are so many ways of finding the truth that it was almost impossible to punish the wrong person. But it would this time.

"Argh!" I pushed myself up and started pacing again. What else did I know? Only what Taria told me. I stopped as If I'd walked into the wall. Interdimensional Law only allowed sentencing when the accused was aware and present.

If I could get away, there would be time. Time to find proof to clear me. Not forever. After all, I'd count as dropped out if I skipped classes for thirty days consecutively.

But how to get out? She said that an alarm would go off if I left the corridor. They couldn't put a spell on me, so it would have to be on the corridor. Was it on the floor? The walls?

There would be a meal brought in two hours. Obviously, I should wait until after that, to give me as much time to get away as possible. If I could figure out a way to escape.

I scanned the room, with a little more interest this time. There was a cot, a table with a pitcher of water and a cup. The cot had a sheet, but no blanket. One window in the room, not particularly big, but big enough in a pinch. Except that there was no curtains, and I was on the third floor. Even with the sheets, there was no way to reach the bottom safely, assuming no one noticed me climbing down the main building on campus. We'll call that plan 'z'.

Something flashed in front of the window, and I pulled back. Then I recognized it, and quickly opened the window. Dragonflies were not a natural occurrence in October in Saskatchewan.

The large insect flew into my room and changed into Denise. Who promptly shut the window again, with a shiver. "Are you okay?"

"Physically? Yes. Everything else?" I shook my head. "Are you going to get in trouble?"

"Locater isn't good enough to pick me up unless I'm badly injured. As long as no one sees me, I'm not here."

"I didn't attack Phyna."

Denise waved a hand like it was inconsequential. "None of us think you did."

"Taria does. She says if I can't prove my innocence tomorrow, I'll be found guilty."

"Yeah, Allison's going through her notes."

I winced. "Will she get in trouble for that?"

"Allison works for Taria. And she says that Taria wants you to disappear. She can't say it or help you, but…"

"Yeah, I figured the same. But how? I can't think of a plan. Can you?"

Denise just smiled.

***

I recognized the security guard who brought me my food. Jostep was a Kayte, teleporters whose skin looks like the night sky. Deep, shiny black with bright white spots. "Hello."

"Hello. Apparently you just can't stay out of trouble, can you?" There was a sad playfulness to the question.

"Apparently not. But I didn't hurt her, I promise."

He shrugged. "Not for me to decide. Trial's tomorrow. Better eat up, you'll need your strength."

"Thank you." He left, acknowledging my thanks with a wave.

My dinner was a couple slices of cheese pizza, probably because they knew for a fact that it was safe for me to eat. I ate slowly, chewing carefully. He had been gone about ten minutes when I finished. I turned out the light, waited another minute, and then waved my glow stone across the window twice.

I opened the door and tried not to jump at the buzzing of the large dragonfly leaving my hair. The corridor was brightly lit, and empty. The dragonfly flew around the corner, then flew back and flew in a wide circle. Telling me to wait.

A minute passed. Another. Sweat started to leak down my neck. This was not going to work. This was an awful plan.

Denise darted back down the hallway and came back, this time flying straight up. I walked towards her. As I got closer, I could hear raised voices. Angry voices.

Kara? Bria? This was their best plan?

"What? Are you crazy? That would be stupid! There is no way that an elemental could trump a Werewolf. Do you know how strong I am?" Kara was shouting.

"Do you know I can freeze you solid, right here, right now?" Bria's voice echoed off the ceiling. I wasn't the only one who needed acting lessons.

Much quieter, I could hear someone trying to calm them down. Tim suddenly appeared from the other side of the corridor, stopping shy of the entrance. Denise shifted back to human size, as Tim carefully reached across and picked me up.

Allison had looked through Taria's notes extensively. Because they couldn't cast any magic on me right now, all magic was on the corridor. There was a barrier at the end of the hallway, but because I wasn't a teleporter or flyer, they only covered the bottom three feet. In addition, there was an unspecific weight spell in place. They had considered that guards and the like might come, so more weight was fine, but if the weight went below a certain limit for longer than a few seconds, someone would check it out. Denise was going to be the decoy weight, turning into a dragonfly to leave in about an hour. Or sooner, if it looked like someone was coming. I prayed she didn't get caught.

Tim was more than strong enough to lift me three feet off the ground, and over the barrier. Being a yeti, he could even see the magic of the barrier. Quickly he maneuvered me, and carried me bridal style to the staircase. Any guards there might have been were busy trying to break up the 'fight' that now had Kara growling and Bria throwing ice around. I really hoped they didn't get in trouble for this.

Ilse met us at the staircase, wearing one of her more concealing dresses and a veil. "Put this on." She helped/forced me into a similar dress and veil. "Walk with me. The way I taught you. Don't speak."

Head up, chin out, I did my best to imitate her glide. Just two vampires on the stairwell, taking precautions from the lights. Tim vanished, after softly clapping a hand on my shoulder and wishing me luck. Probably to signal Kara and Bria to reign it in before they got in major trouble. And because eight foot plus yetis are very noticeable, even at Hyde. A couple of vampires are not.

We continued all the way down, to the door that led to the underground levels. Krystal was waiting there. She joined us as we continued through the first level, the second, and the door of the third. "Adrian's waiting on the other side. He's the only one whose mind Taria can't read."

I nodded. "Thank you. All of you. I know you're all taking risks for helping me. I really don't want anyone getting in trouble over me."

Ilse helped me take off the dress and veil. "It was nothing. Take care. We will prove your innocence, but you *must _not_ be found*."

"Once you're through, I'll freeze the door. That

will give you some time on the off chance something goes wrong and they do realize you're gone," Krystal said. "Be careful."

"I will."

Adrian was indeed waiting, with my backpack. "How did you get that?"

"You left your window open. Denise flew in, found it, tossed it out, flew out, put it on and walked away. No one noticed. Now, follow me."

I had thought the path to the cavern was convoluted, but it was nothing compared to this. A few times, we couldn't even walk; we had to crawl through tunnels that were too small to stand in. Then we came to water.

"You can swim, right?" Adrian put my backpack in a waterproof bag, and indicated I should follow him. "If you can't, say something now."

"Are you crazy?"

"Probably. This way. You have to go down." He jumped in.

Yeah, follow Adrian, who was a dark blur in daytime, through the dark, and then underwater where there were no lights. Great plan. Still, he'd led me straight this far. With a deep breath, I jumped in after him.

The water was cold enough that I thought I was

getting frostbite. All the air I had taken was forced out of me. I surfaced long enough to take another breath, then went back underwater.

I couldn't see a thing. Where was he? Where was I supposed to go? Waves. I could feel movement in the water. Not having a better plan, I followed it.

Then I hit my head on a wall. Down, he said to go down. I resurfaced for another breath, then hand on the wall, I forced myself to go further down.

I found a passage in the wall and managed to swim through it, only hitting walls or scraping myself up three times. The cold made each pain hurt worse. My bones were becoming icicles. Air, I needed air! Where was Adrian?

A hand grabbed me and pulled up. I kicked off, and made surface. "Where are we?" I gasped.

"C'mon. There's ground here." I heard a thump. My bag hitting ground? Then there was light. It was a room, a furnished room. Fancy furniture, too. A bed, chairs, and a table. Most importantly, there were steps out of the water.

"What is this?" I asked, climbing out of the frigid pool.

"Far as I can tell? It was ambassador guest quarters that the merpeople used before the school was founded. I don't think anyone even remembers that it's here. No one, other than me, has been here in years. Here." He waved what looked to be a large shell made of gold over me. I was suddenly warm and dry. I loved that shell. It was my favorite piece of technology ever. Whoever invented it was a genius. Then he waved it over himself.

"How did you even find this?"

"Exploring. Lots of exploring." He waved to a door that I hadn't noticed, because it matched the rocky walls so well. "That's a bathroom. Everything works, and the water is potable. Food is a little trickier, but we have a plan." He walked to the table and put his hand on a silver colored box about the size of a small safe.

"This is an extremely secure, usually only used for government purposes, way of transporting messages and parcels. They come in linked sets of two. What you put in one, goes to the other. Allison has one, and this one is mine. We can deliver food, messages, and other small things to you that way."

"Wow, that's pretty cool." I examined the box. "But you know this is just a stop-gap measure. I *have* to prove that I'm innocent and get back to classes. The sooner the better."

"We know." Adrian rubbed at his forehead. "But we have thirty days. Surely we can come up with something by then."

I tried to smile. They were all so kind to do this for me, especially with the risks. "I won't be able to see anyone until this is over, will I?"

"Not any of the others. Someone could take your

location from their mind. Even if you met them somewhere else, if someone read that they had seen you, they'd be in trouble. And I can't come too often, or it could lead someone here."

"Right, don't go getting in trouble. I don't want anyone getting in trouble." I winced. "Do you think they'll be alright?"

"They'll be fine." He gave me a half smile and started inspecting the room, probably for the umpteenth time.

"Adrian?"

He looked at me, green eyes reflecting the light. "Yes?"

"Tell me everything will be alright?"

"It will. We'll figure out what happened, prove your innocence, and find out why Phyna would do this. You'll be back before you know it."

Well, I couldn't be mad at him for lying if I told him to do so. "Then, I'll be alright here." It was just as much a lie. "Try to hurry, will you? It's going to be a very boring month otherwise."

Coming Soon!

The Hyde Chronicles: Book Four

Rooked

By H. J. Harding

The clock is ticking. Thirty days to find the truth. Thirty days to find the proof. Forces beyond what anyone was expecting come into play. Trust is threatened as even Violet and her allies cannot tell each other all they know. Failure could mean the end of all they know. But is success even possible?

Coming Soon!

www.ingramcontent.com/pod-product-compliance
Lightning Source LLC
Chambersburg PA
CBHW070859180626
46817CB00003B/836